Tracie McBride is a New Zealander who lives in Melbourne, Australia with her husband and three children. Her work has appeared or is forthcoming in over 80 print and electronic publications, including the Stoker Award-nominated anthologies *Horror for Good* and *Horror Library Volume 5*. Her debut collection *Ghosts Can Bleed* contains much of the work that earned her a Sir Julius Vogel Award, and her work has been shortlisted for the Aurealis Awards and the Shadows Awards.

Visitors to her blog are welcome at:

http://traciemcbridewriter.wordpress.com/.

T0118837

Drive, She Said

and other stories

A short story collection
by Tracie McBride

This is a work of fiction. The events and characters portrayed herein are imaginary and are not intended to refer to specific places, events or living persons. The opinions expressed in this manuscript are solely the opinions of the author and do not necessarily represent the opinions of the publisher.

IFWG Publishing International
Melbourne

www.ifwgpublishing.com

To my youngest daughter, Zoe. Kia kaha.

Table of Contents

Breaking Windows

They say that the eyes are the windows to the soul. And what do burglars do when they can't get in through a locked door?

They go in through a window.

Initial reports placed the rate of possession at one in one thousand. I didn't think that was bad odds; in a city of five million people, that meant only five thousand possessed. One small suburb. As long as it wasn't my suburb, I could cope with that.

The first possessed person I saw was on TV. "The images you are about to see may be disturbing to some," warned a solemn faced presenter. The camera cut to a young man in his early twenties cuffed to a wall by his wrists and ankles. A fifth restraint around his neck was supposed to keep his head still, stop him from hurting himself, but it wasn't working; his head whipped from side to side so fast it was a blur. He had bitten his tongue, and blood sprayed out in all directions, splattering against the stark white wall behind him. And all the while this incredible sound issued from his lips. One minute it was a stream of obscenities uttered in guttural tones at odds with his youthful appearance, next he was speaking in tongues, next he sang a wordless song so high pitched it verged on inaudible, next he wept like a brutalised child.

Someone off camera extended a long metal rod into the frame and used it to lift the possessed man's shirt up to his neck. The camera zoomed in to show the words being etched by an invisible hand onto his chest and belly in shallow scratches that slowly welled with blood.

Well
Slut
Nigh
Home
Crow

The words were random, without context, yet I felt compelled to stare at them, as if I were on the verge of decoding their meaning.

The camera panned out again, the better to show the viewer how he arched his back and bent his limbs into impossible angles, until I was sure we were about to see his bones stick out through his skin. Still spouting gibberish, he stopped shaking his head and faced directly forward. His face twisted into a hateful caricature of himself. But his eyes…through them, you could still see the human imprisoned inside. They were terrified, agonized, pleading—

They were broken.

Leo didn't tell me he was going in for ocular prostheses. He said he was being sent on a week-long training course, which was only a partial lie. The first four days of his absence were spent recovering from the operation to remove and replace his perfectly good eyes. The next three really were taken up by a training course to teach him how to most effectively operate his new ones. When he came home, we fought, which in our household meant that he talked and I sulked in silence.

"They're state of the art. They have all sorts of advanced functions. I can even use them as X-rays. Most importantly, they're fitted with DSDs—demonic spectrum detectors. I can literally see the devil inside people," he said, and—

"The Bureau paid for it all, it didn't cost us a cent," and—

"I had no choice. I had to get them. It's a requirement of my job," and—

"I can protect you with these eyes. You and the children we are going to have. You must know, I did it all for you,", and—

"You don't want me to get possessed, do you? 'Cos this is the only way we know of to stop the demons from getting in," and—

"I couldn't tell you beforehand, because I knew you'd react like this," and—

"You'll get used to them, Jess. Just give it time."

He used to have such beautiful eyes. They would change colour according to his mood, and I used to joke that they were like those rings you could buy in bargain basement shops when we were kids. These new ones were big and bulbous and mirrored. They were a piece of military hardware, so it was little wonder that the designers had not taken aesthetics into consideration.

"You look like an insect," I said, when I could finally bring myself to speak. "Where are your eyelids?" He laughed, took me into his arms, and kissed me on the top of my head.

"These babies,"—he tapped his fingernails against his new eyeballs, making a metallic clink, and I flinched—"don't need constant lubrication. My eyelids wouldn't fit over them anyway, so they did away with them altogether. If I want to close my eyes, I just do this." Grey screens slid horizontally across his eyes with a barely audible mechanical whir. His windows were well and truly boarded up.

We ended the argument the way we always did, by making love, but only after he agreed to wear sunglasses to bed. It made no difference to Leo—he could now see in the dark. Even with his eyes obscured with shades, I kept my own tightly shut.

I tracked the worsening statistics obsessively. One in nine hundred. One in seven hundred and fifty. One in six hundred. One in five hundred. Everyone had a story to tell, knew someone who knew someone who had been possessed. The church attempted to perform exorcisms, but more often than not they ended in the maiming or death of either the possessed person or the exorcist. And even if they had been entirely successful, there simply weren't enough qualified priests to make a dent in the problem.

The media reported the calamities. Mental health facilities burned to the ground by zealots mistaking mental illness for possession. Terrified citizens barricading themselves in their homes and slowly starving to death. White supremacist groups taking advantage of the confusion to conduct ethnic cleansing programmes in the name of "driving out the demons". The danger, once so remote, now seemed to press in on all sides.

Leo got a promotion, which was Bureau-speak for "a little more money and a lot more work." He headed up a DED (Demonic Entities Detection) squad, and regularly put in eighteen-hour days. Had he still possessed the eyes he'd been born with, I would have been able to see the fatigue and desperation in them when he stumbled in past midnight. Instead, I had to rely on the slump of his shoulders and the gravel in his voice for clues to his wellbeing.

Leo wasn't supposed to tell me, but he had to unload on someone; what the media didn't show was what happened to all the possessed citizens that the DED squad rounded up. Row upon row of incessantly thrashing and cursing bodies chained to hospital beds, with the beds themselves chained to the floor to stop them from levitating. And it was Leo's job to do the chaining.

It still wasn't clear if the demonic plague, as it had become known, was contagious, and they couldn't find any staff brave enough to find out. If you had a shitload of money and a concerned relative or two, or some hefty Catholic connections, then maybe, just maybe, you'd be exorcised. Otherwise, the possessed were being left where they lay to rot in their own filth. The optically enhanced, like Leo, were too valuable to waste playing nursemaid to a bunch of meat shells. That's what Bureau staff called them — meat shells. As if the entities inside those poor people were nothing more menacing than a hermit crab. I knew Leo had to find a way to put some distance between himself and his work, but his callousness frightened me more than the demons did.

Sometimes I woke up in the middle of the night to feel the bed beside me empty. I could sense Leo standing awake in the shadows, watching me.

Just watching me.

One in four hundred. One in three hundred. One in two hundred and fifty.

"You need ocular implants too."

"No."

"We'll get a second mortgage. You can pick up some extra shifts—that should be easy enough to do, they're dropping like flies at the salon."

"Fewer staff, but fewer customers too. No, I won't do it."

"Come on, Jess. Sooner or later, they're going to get you. This is the only way."

"I'll quit my job instead. Stay home. Lock all the doors."

"You know that's no guarantee. Listen, I can probably pull some strings at the Bureau. Get you bumped up the waiting list. Maybe even get a discount."

"No."

"The new civilian models don't look half bad. Couple of the guys' wives have them. If you'd just..."

"I. Said. No."

It was Leo's turn to fall silent then. No conciliatory lovemaking to follow—radiating anger, he turned his back to me in bed. Then—

"You remember Tim from work?" His voice was muffled, as if he were speaking into his pillow.

"Vaguely..."

"Remember I told you about his crazy ex-girlfriend? The one that took a baseball bat to his car after they broke up? Well, he went to her house yesterday. Picked her up and took her into a detention centre."

"She was possessed?"

"That's the thing. She wasn't possessed, though you'd be hard pressed to tell the difference, the way she carries on with her foul mouth and violent outbursts. No, he just said that she was. He's the one with the DSDs embedded in his face, so who's going to argue with him?"

You could have argued, I thought. I edged away from him. "Why are you telling me this?"

I felt him shrug. "I dunno... When good blokes like Tim do shit like that, and blokes like me let him do it... Things are getting bad, Jess. Really bad."

One in two hundred. One in one hundred and fifty. One in one hundred. Fifty thousand people possessed in our city. They no longer bothered restraining them in hospital beds, just herded them into hastily constructed concrete bunkers and bolted the doors shut.

At first I thought it was the stress that was making me throw up every morning. After a week of it, Leo pointed out the bleeding obvious.

"Jess, honey…you could be pregnant."

A home test kit confirmed it. As I stared at the stick, Leo reached out and stroked my arm with a feather-light touch as if he was afraid I might break.

"I know we've talked about this before, but…you really should reconsider getting prostheses."

I imagined being entombed in one of those bunkers with hundreds of other filthy, tortured, gibbering meat shells, my baby—*our* baby—kicking inside me. I took a deep, shuddering breath and nodded.

"OK. You're right. Book me in."

I got the stock standard civilian model; it was all we could afford. No X-ray vision, no DSDs, just a lifetime guarantee of protection from demonic possession. Oh, and 20/20 vision, of course.

"The default setting of your new eyes is closed," the nurse said as he peeled the bandages off my head, "so don't be alarmed if you see nothing at first. Just imagine consciously blinking. That will activate the mechanism that will open your eyes."

I did as I was told. And was immediately struck with how unchanged everything looked from when I had last gazed on the world with flesh eyes. Colours, shapes, distance, perspective, all was as it should be. I had to admit, the manufacturers had done a superb job. Apart from the dull throbbing at the back of my new eyeballs, I wouldn't have known I'd been operated on.

Until I looked in the mirror.

Without the extra features, my implants were smaller and less protruding than Leo's. But I could not get past their colourless reflective surface or the absence of sclera. I would have cried, but I no longer could.

It wasn't a possessed person, but a common garden variety psycho-path that killed Leo. Snuck up behind him while he was on curfew patrol and got in one unlucky hit on the back of his head with a tyre iron before the rest of the squad took him down. Technically, it was manslaughter; the blow itself did not kill Leo, so his friends told me, but it was enough to damage and dislodge his helmet. The impact of his skull on the footpath when he fell finished him off. It was a fact that the offender's lawyer would have exploited to the full, had he made it into a court room.

"Don't worry, Jessica," his colleagues said, "we took care of the bastard for you."

One in eighty. One in sixty-five. One in forty. Their assurances were cold comfort.

Even if I had been able to contact his family, all interstate travel had been banned in the newly imposed state of civil emergency. So besides me, only Bureau personnel and their spouses attended Leo's funeral. They all sported various models of ocular prostheses. From the nose down, they grieved, shoulders heaving, mouths contorted in sobs. But from the nose up—nothing.

The funeral director invited us all to join him in a brief prayer. Fifty-seven heads tipped forward in perfunctory bows. Fifty-seven pairs of artificial eyes closed. I kept mine open and raised my hand to block out the lower half of my field of vision. With their eyes veiled in flat grey shutters and the rest of their faces obscured, they looked more inhuman than ever.

I shifted uncomfortably on my feet. I'd been experiencing niggling little pains all morning. The baby was restless too; I breathed shallowly as she executed a slow roll inside me, my belly visibly undulating under my snug maternity shirt. Another pain, sharper this time, and a gush of warm wetness spilled down my legs.

My waters had broken.

The most frightening thing about the possessed, besides the prospect of becoming one of them, was their unpredictability. Although some were a danger only to themselves, you couldn't keep a beloved family member chained up in your home for fear that he or she would turn on you without warning. The demons had become stronger, had learned how to drive their meat shells more effectively, and they could make their host bodies do improbable things. I heard reports of possessed gnawing off their own hands to escape from handcuffs. In the house opposite mine, one of the occupants was possessed overnight, unbeknownst to the rest of the family. The next morning the front of the house was strung with human organs and intestines, like a macabre parody of Christmas decorations. If somebody close to you became possessed, you had little choice but to turn them out and lock the door behind you.

One in thirty. One in twenty-five. One in eighteen.

One in ten.

Half a million people in our city alone, possessed by demons. Half a million people screaming, roaring, bleeding, contorting, roaming the streets while the unpossessed cowered behind their barricades and waited for their food supplies to run out. If you didn't already have ocular implants like mine, you were out of luck; even if you had the money, and even if you could make it through the press of meat shells between you and the hospital, the waiting lists were two years long.

I looked out through a chink in the boards across my window and saw a possessed child for the first time. He couldn't have been more than three years old. He sat in the street with his chubby little legs outstretched, chanting obscenity-laced nursery rhymes in an adult's voice and rhythmically stabbing his thighs over and over again with a box cutter clutched in his fist. Blood pooled beneath him and trickled into the drain. He looked up at me and laughed, a deep, throaty maniacal laugh that should not have been able to come from such a small child.

But he had such beautiful eyes.

I looked down at my baby daughter in her cot. Chloe had just woken up, and she cooed and gurgled to me, pedalling her legs beneath the covers and reaching up to be held. I leaned over and quickly swaddled her tight in her blankets then lifted her out of the cot and laid her gently on the floor. I kneeled behind her and clamped my knees either side of her head to hold her still.

She squirmed against her restraints and whimpered a little, then quietened, fascinated by the glint of light off the knife I held above her face. My hand shook, and I felt phantom tears sliding down my cheeks. Sensing my distress, Chloe began to cry.

I thought of the boy outside. Then I pinned her eyelid open and slid the knife in.

The Truth About Dolphins

"Look! I can see a fin!"

The cry goes up from the bow, and all the tourists rush to see. Another fin slices through the water, then another, until soon the sea ahead of them is studded with a dozen fins. The skipper turns off the motor, allowing the boat to float to a stop several metres away from the school. Mina hangs back; no need to join the crush at the front of the boat when the school will be hanging around here for a little while yet. She can read it in the lazy movements of the dolphins, knows it with a certainty in her gut, although how she came by this knowledge, she cannot say.

"Bottlenose dolphins," their tour guide, Ingrid, says. "We're in luck!" Ingrid's skin is rough and deeply tanned, her hair white-blonde and straw-like from exposure to sun, salt and wind. She's around Mina's age at a guess, a sturdily built woman dressed in khakis as if she is on the African plains instead of on a tourist boat in the Bay of Islands.

"We'll just observe them for a few minutes," Ingrid says, "and if there are no infants with the school, then you'll be able to get in the water with them." A buzz of excitement runs through the thirty-odd other customers on board. Mina pretends to look for baby dolphins along with the rest of them, but she already knows; the youngest dolphin amongst them is a strapping four-year-old adolescent, the next birth in the school not due for another five months. The dolphins talk to her, not in whistles and squeaks — that form of communication is reserved for their own species — but in the flick of a tail, the tilt of a dorsal fin, the intricate swim patterns that appear random to everybody else. They have been calling to her for weeks now, the message garbled by distance, her sleep disturbed with a sensation akin to a psychic itch.

Mina's boyfriend, Aaron, leans in and speaks close into her ear. The casual observer would see his supportive hand under her elbow, a loving smile projected to the world, never knowing the hand gripped tightly enough to bruise, that the smile concealed savage intent. "Still don't get what all the fuss is about…they're just a bunch of fucking fish. If these Conservation pussies weren't around, I'd spear one and fillet it for dinner." He's just trying to get a rise out of her; he knows perfectly well that dolphins are mammals, not fish. A miasma of alcohol fumes infuses his breath and emanates from his skin, the residue from the night before.

"Don't know what all the fuss is about…and yet you're still here," she replies. It's brave of her to talk back; Aaron is a mean drunk, and even meaner hung over. "I still don't know why you bought us the tickets if you think this is such a waste of time."

But she does know, just as he knew that one truth about dolphins. It's part of his M.O.—showering her with gifts one minute, the next refusing to let her enjoy them, keeping her constantly off balance and unsure of herself. In some ways, Aaron's a lot like a dolphin in his courtship rituals; friendly and playful at first, but once he sets his sights on a mate, turning sinister. Isolating her from the rest of her "school"…sticking relentlessly by her side…smacking her around if she tries to get away.

Ingrid is talking to the group, and Mina focuses on her, pointedly ignoring Aaron who seethes silently next to her.

"…ancient Maori believed that dolphins were the messengers of the gods and that they could foretell the future by the way they jumped out of the water." Two dreadlocked young German women nod fervently at this. As if on cue, two dolphins leap in unison and re-enter the water with a splash that saturates Ingrid down one side. The crowd laughs and claps, and an elderly American couple mutter of a conspiracy. "They're not really wild, they're really circus trained and sent to perform tricks for us. I bet they swim back into their cages right after we leave."

"What do you reckon that message from the gods was, aye?" Aaron says, nudging Mina a little too hard so she stumbles on the damp floor of the gently rocking boat. Another passenger nearby snickers at her apparent clumsiness. "I reckon they were telling us that this bitch is full of shit." He jerks a thumb in Ingrid's direction. "Oh, but I forgot—you believe in all that mumbo jumbo, don't you?"

Mina is all too familiar with this game. She may have scored the first point, but he would not rest until she was beaten and bloody—figuratively or literally. He stares at her, hard, challenging her to respond, but she does not answer or meet his eyes, her stomach turning in slow rolls at the prospect of conflict. Left with nothing to push against, he eventually turns away with a contemptuous sneer.

"Ok, folks," Ingrid says, "looks like it's all clear, so those of you who want to get in the water can put on wetsuits and flippers."

A young girl, maybe nine or ten years old, starts to sniffle. She has been fearful and whiny the whole trip—What if the boat crashes? What if it sinks? What if they get lost and can't find their way back to dry land?—and she tugs on her mother's sleeve, whispering something in her ear. The mother shakes her head, then straightens and says to Ingrid in a crisp British accent, "There aren't any sharks out here, are there? You know, because of the dolphins."

"Actually, that's a myth," Ingrid replies. "Sharks and dolphins often occupy the same waters. Where you see dolphins feeding on the surface, there will usually be sharks feeding near the bottom."

A nervous titter ripples through the group. Some people hesitate, shooting second glances at the wetsuits in their hands, and the girl's sniffles turn into outright howls. Ingrid grins maliciously, and Mina snorts. She's not sure who she's more annoyed at...Ingrid for trying to put the wind up everyone, or the other passengers for their paranoia. She approaches the girl.

"Do you know what else the ancient Maori believed?" she asks, not condescending to bend down to the child but addressing her as if she is a very small adult.

"N-n-no," the girl stammers. "What?"

"They believed that sharks were guardian spirits," Mina says. "If you were out at sea and in trouble, you could call on a shark to save you."

"But…but sharks eat people," the girl says, conflict writ large on her tear-streaked face.

Mina shrugs. "Yeah…sometimes they do. Maybe that's only if you don't deserve to be saved."

She leaves the girl to think it over and goes back to Aaron, who has been watching the exchange through narrowed eyes.

"You're good with kids," he says. It sounds more like an accusation than a compliment. "I can't wait to see what you're like with our kids."

She makes a noncommittal noise and looks away. The thought of any child of hers having Aaron for a father makes her ill, as does his smug certainty that she will be his brood mare.

Ingrid comes over to them. "Are you getting in?" she says, proffering them wetsuits. Aaron waves her away dismissively.

"Yes," says Mina, "but I don't need a wetsuit. I have my togs on under my clothes."

"Are you sure?" Ingrid says, looking Mina up and down. "The water can be deceptively cold, even at this time of year. Especially if you're intending to stay in for more than a few minutes."

"I'm sure," she replies. "I'm a big girl; if I get too cold I can always get out."

"Well, OK…" Ingrid walks away, sparing Mina one last dubious backward glance before returning her attention to other customers.

Mina undresses, kicking off her sandals then peeling away her jeans and T-shirt. She has chosen to wear her skimpiest bikini, a crocheted little red number that only just stops short of indecent exposure. She is suddenly, acutely aware of the four young Aussie blokes, here on a post-uni backpacking holiday. And they are acutely aware of her. One of them pauses with one leg in his wetsuit and almost unbalances, he is gawping so much.

"What the fuck?" Aaron mutters under his breath. "I thought

I told you never to wear that in public." One of the Aussies, a tall, powerfully built man with close-cropped dark hair, pushes off the railing he has been leaning against and comes closer.

"Cool tatt," he says, indicating the small artwork she has inked to the left of her belly button. "I like those tribal designs." He pushes one shoulder forward, the better to display the tribal band tattooed around one impressive bicep. Leaning over, he squints, pretending not to be able to make out the details, then kneels in front of her, his mouth dangerously close to her bare skin. It is a provocative gesture, reeking of sex and submission, and Aaron bristles. He wouldn't dare start anything though, she thinks, not a man of that size, not with his three mates there to back him up, and the way the man smirks up at Aaron in a lazy challenge, the Aussie has that all figured out. But Aaron would want to punish someone for the affront; Mina would no doubt shoulder the blame for leading the guy on. She closes her eyes for a moment, feeling the warmth of the young man's breath on her belly.

"Dolphin, yeah?" He looks up at her expectantly. The first of the wetsuit-clad tourists have entered the water; squeals of delight, curiously edged with anxiety, rise up as the dolphins skim ever closer, ever faster to the humans.

She does not answer. She reaches up and unties her bikini at the neck, letting the top fall, then slides the bottoms to her feet. The startled Australian gets up, and she presses against him, sending him backpedalling to the boat railing. The dolphins thrash about in the water with a sudden burst of activity, as if they are under attack. She clasps her hands behind the man's neck and draws on the dolphins' frenetic energy to maintain her momentum and push him over the side, his weight carrying her over with him. The water closes over her head, muting the noises—shocked gasps, bawdy cheers from the Aussies and an enraged roar from Aaron—and it is all she can do not to draw a deep, calming breath.

Mina and the Australian surface at the same time, and the dark-haired stranger has only an instant to cast a befuddled look at her before Aaron dives in between them.

"You filthy slut…" he spits.

"Hey, steady on, mate," the Aussie says, placing a hand on Aaron's shoulder. Aaron shrugs it off, a gesture made awkward and extravagant by his need to simultaneously tread water. He swings a wild punch that somehow still manages to connect with his would-be rival. The man yelps as blood bursts from his nose.

Then Aaron fixes both hands around Mina's neck and drags her down.

He presses his face close to hers, almost as if he intends to kiss her. The water, the too-close perspective, his fury, all distorts his features, fixing them into a monstrous mask she has only glimpsed before. Perhaps, she thinks, it is not a mask but his true face uncovered. His grip is merciless; her lungs would soon be burning with a lack of oxygen even if she weren't underwater. The pain is compelling, yet she turns her mind from it. There is still so much to enjoy in this moment. The chilling caress of the sea on her naked body. The blood dispersing through the water and tinting it a pretty shade of pink. The graceful movements of the dolphins that now encircle them, observing them as if they were staging some kind of underwater performance for the sea mammals' entertainment. She recalls the American couple's theory—they're not really wild, they're really circus trained and sent to perform tricks for us—and smiles. Distantly, she registers splashes and shouts as more passengers, presumably the Aussie boys come to help their mate, jump into the sea. But if they have any thought of helping her, they have no hope of getting through the dolphin audience.

Then the dolphins turn in unison and swim down and away from them. Their message is clear, and although she has been expecting it, she tenses in anticipation of what is to come.

At first, the creature is little more than a dark shadow far beneath her feet. A dark shadow that moves with incredible speed, growing larger by the moment until it resolves into the grey-blue form of a mako shark. She—the dolphins told Mina it would be a she—is big for her species, pushing four metres long. She turns slightly on her side as she circles the couple, flashing the white skin of her belly.

Bubbles stream from Aaron's mouth as he lets out an under-water scream. He releases his grip on Mina's neck and puts his hands out in front of him in a pitiful attempt at self-defence. The shark slows and opens her mouth wide, showing off multiple rows of blade-like teeth, and Aaron shudders. A cloud of yellow urine billows from between his legs.

Far from being flat and emotionless—like a psychopath's, as she has heard them described—the mako's eyes seem almost genial. *Go ahead,* she seems to say, *take a breath. I'll wait for you.* Mina complies, propelling herself to the surface with two strong kicks and dragging in great lungfuls of salty, summer air. She glances towards the boat. The last of the swimmers is clambering up the side to safety, clumsy in his panic, and the dolphins, their job done, are nowhere to be seen. Ingrid gestures at her frantically—get out, get out!—and the little girl is wide-eyed and frozen, her terror rendering her immoveable despite her mother's best efforts to turn her face away from the inevitable carnage.

Mina dives back beneath the surface. The giant fish takes hold of Aaron with an odd gentleness, slowly closing her fearsome jaws on his torso and arms like a bird dog retrieving her master's kill. Mina shakes her head in dismay; she knew the shark had been coming, but somehow she had naively thought it was just going to scare Aaron, not, not...

Shark and woman eye each other silently.

Why didn't you just leave?

And that has always been an option. Go into a women's refuge, quit the job that she loves, move away from the few supportive friends she has left, and leave Aaron to make good on his threat to hurt her family if she ever tried to break up with him again. And then, all too soon, he would move on to another victim, while Mina scraped together the remnants of her tattered life.

The shark makes the decision for her. Aaron has passed out, through terror or lack of air, which is a blessing, she thinks, because he will not feel the mako's teeth as she closes her jaws, piercing his flesh and crushing his limp body. With a flick of her powerful tail, the fish dives out of sight, taking Aaron with her.

Mina resurfaces and swims back to the boat. What seems

like a hundred pairs of hands reach over the side to haul her up, and a hundred voices yammer in her ears. In the background, a strident American voice threatens to sue. She catches the eye of the British girl, who is still wide-eyed and open-mouthed, but no longer with fear; the girl's gaze flicks from the unharmed swimmer to the now tranquil sea and back again, comprehension slowly forming. Mina offers a tiny, grim-faced nod, and the girl mirrors her, sealing the secret between them.

Mina shivers uncontrollably from the cold, although the others will probably think it is shock, and someone envelops her in an oversized beach towel and draws her into a protective embrace. It is the dark-haired Aussie. *Could he be another dolphin?* she thinks, and almost laughs despite the traumatic situation; she never could tell until it was too late. She mutters thanks to him and pulls away. Beneath the towel, she brushes her fingertips over her tattoo.

Not a dolphin; it is a shark. Her guardian spirit.

Wooden Heart

The Mandragora had been Raisa's companion for as long as she could remember. She knew the stories, had been told them time and time again, of how its seed had been planted on the day of her conception. The tree's first shoots had broken the surface of the earth on the day she was born, and from then on it had grown as she had grown.

"Talk to it," the Sisters had urged her, and so she had, every day she was able. She had offered it her first babbling words, and it had seemed to listen, gently nodding its fronds towards her. It had been easy to imagine it alive back then; its rounded protuberances did so resemble her own chubby limbs, and her childish imagination furnished it with eyes, a nose, a smiling curve of a mouth.

When she grew old enough, it fell to Raisa to care for the Mandragora. She watered it, fertilised it, and kept its leaves free from parasites. She attended the convent school with the other privileged daughters of the city, but none of them shared her rarity of status. In the classroom, the other girls paid her more respect than they did the teacher; in the playground, she was shunned. The tree became more than just her duty; it became her only friend. She whispered all her secrets to it, and longed for the day when it would become flesh and be able to respond. Occasionally a Sister would check on the condition of the tree, but for the most part they left her alone to commune with it.

"You and the Mandragora are both the product of generations of selective breeding," the Sisters told her. "There have never been others like you, nor will there likely be again. Your union will be wondrous, and together you will wield tremendous power, such as the world has never known." Even as a child, Raisa understood the unspoken message; the Sisters would truly wield the power, not her. She and her tree-spouse would merely be the conduits.

They reminded her constantly of the imperative for her to remain pure. Pure, clean, untouched…she did not understand what they meant, not yet, only that she did not feel pure. Not with dirt permanently ingrained into the skin of her knees from spending so much time kneeling amongst the Mandragora's roots.

As she grew taller, so did the Mandragora, matching her inch for inch. Just like Raisa, it thinned out as it lengthened. Its trunk bifurcated upside down, giving the appearance of two wooden legs. It grew shapely and strong and its twin branches stretched out either side of it as if to snatch the sunlight from the sky. Raisa began to develop into a woman, sprouting little buds of breasts. The Mandragora had always had a tiny tumescence at the junction of the split in its trunk, and as the bulge expanded, it grew a modest apron of leaves to cover it, not unlike the hair beginning to cover Raisa's private parts. Curious, Raisa lifted the leaves to see what was evolving beneath them, until one of the Sisters caught her and slapped her hand away.

"But why?" Raisa demanded. "You have always pressed me to be close to it. It is my betrothed. Why may I not touch it and witness it growing like I always have?"

"You are not a child any longer, Raisa. Your time grows near. Soon enough you will know the Mandragora intimately, but until then, you must learn to practice some modesty."

The explanation left her more confused than ever. For reasons she could not identify, Raisa's cheeks grew hot, and she did not press for more. Modesty. Shame. Intimacy. More words whose meanings eluded her. She began to avoid the tree, even resent it a little, and spent hours sulking in her chambers until the Sisters sought her out and chivvied her back into service.

Alone with the Mandragora, she squinted at it. How had she ever been able to see at as a person? It was just a tree. A still, silent, rough-barked and faceless tree. Its leaves stirred in the afternoon breeze, as if it had read her mind and was trying to communicate with her. She knew that at the right time she was meant to couple with it, to bring it to sentient life and human form, but in her ignorance she could not begin to comprehend the mechanics of the act, much less the magic. She shook her head and turned away.

It was while she was weeding one day that she saw him. A hole, barely big enough to admit her little finger, had developed in the wall surrounding the courtyard, and Raisa sat idly picking at it, worrying at the mortar with a twig until it was big enough for her to spy through. She pressed her eye to the hole…

And jumped back, startled by the sight of a boy—no, a young man—leaning over with his hands on his knees and peering back at her. More tentatively, she approached the hole again. From where she sat she could see the front gate of the convent. The young man had already moved away from the wall. He had picked up a large black leather bag and stood dutifully behind an older gentleman who was deep in conversation with one of the Sisters. A merchant and his servant, perhaps, or a tradesman and his apprentice. The older man turned to say something to the younger one, and he replied. Raisa could not quite make out his words, but the rich, silken timbre of his voice carried on the breeze. The two men passed through the gate into the reception area of the convent, but not before the younger one looked back at Raisa and winked.

Raisa spun away from the hole and leaned against the wall, her heart thumping wildly. She had only glimpsed him for seconds, yet his image was seared into her memory. Such a pale expressive face, such glittering blue eyes, such an abundance of soft blond hair so carelessly restrained at the nape of his neck, such finely turned fingers that would surely raise goose bumps all over her body if he were to brush them over her bare skin… He was simply the most beautiful creature she had ever seen. He moved, he breathed, he smiled, he spoke.

He was nothing like her betrothed.

The Sisters would not allow her to so much as stand in the

same room as a man, let alone speak to one. But her years of solitary exploring meant that she knew the layout of the convent better than they did. Every unlocked door, every dusty hidden passageway, every forgotten storage room—if there was a place for her to hide that would bring her close to the object of her desire, she would find it.

The pair, Raisa learned, were a physician and his son come to attend to one of the Sisters who had fallen down some stairs and broken her leg. Raisa hurried through the labyrinthine corridors until she reached the one that backed onto the infirmary and pressed her ear against the door.

The break was a bad one and had to be reset. While the doctor manipulated the bone and the Sister screamed in pain, the young man attempted to soothe her with words spoken in a low, earnest tone. Raisa imagined that same voice whispering words of love in her ear, and felt suddenly feverish.

The sister's cries ebbed, the authoritative tones of the doctor's voice drowning her out as he issued instructions for her care. "Excuse me," she heard the young man say, "may I use the privy?"

She ducked out of sight around a corner and waited, counting heart beats, until she felt confident there were no Sisters in attendance. Cautiously she stepped back into the corridor.

He stood in front of her, smiling slightly. She gave a startled squeak.

"You're the girl I saw behind the wall, aren't you?" She gave no response. Unfazed, he extended his hand.

"My name is Jonas," he said.

"Raisa," she mumbled. She clasped his hand in hers, fervently hoping that he didn't notice her tremble. His fingers were warm and smooth, just as she had imagined they would be. Jonas looked over his shoulder at the door from which he'd emerged.

"They're expecting me back any minute," he said. "How can I see you again?"

You can't, she wanted to say, but she found herself instead articulating the plan that until now had existed only in her fantasies.

It took some time, and a return visit from Jonas to check on the patient, during which they orchestrated another brief clandestine meeting in the corridor. But, in the end, they executed the plan swiftly, and with a precision born of determination and desire. A powerful sleeping draught, supplied by Jonas and slipped by Raisa into the tea of the Sister on guard duty for the night, a stolen key, a grappling hook and a rope ladder, and a section of the courtyard wall obscured with overgrown vines, and he was over the wall and in her arms.

There were no words of endearment whispered in her ear. He kissed her briefly and savagely, then laid her down at the foot of the Mandragora. Its roots dug into her back. She wriggled about to find a more comfortable position, and Jonas, mistaking her movement for encouragement, hoisted up her skirts and entered her.

It hurt. She buried her face in his neck, stifling her cries. She clung to him, gasping through the pain, enduring it, for this must be the price of love. A new sensation began to insinuate itself, but before it could supplant the pain, Jonas stiffened, groaned, and collapsed on top of her.

And all the while the Mandragora bore witness.

Jonas rolled off her, and they both lay panting at the stars for a time until they regained their breath. What now, Raisa thought frantically, what now? This must be what the Sisters had been warning her about and protecting her against all these years. She could not go to the Mandragora in this state of defilement. She would have to leave the convent, climb over the wall with Jonas and go far, far away.

Jonas chuckled. His fingertips trailed carelessly over her thigh.

"They talk of you outside these walls, you know. They say that there is a young woman of such unsurpassed loveliness that none may gaze on her without falling instantly and irrevocably in love, and that the Sisters keep her cloistered away lest she drive the men of the city mad with desire. Of course, when I heard the story, I had to see for myself if it were true. I could never resist a challenge."

Raisa's skin prickled with foreboding. "That's not why they keep me locked away," she said. "The truth is... I am promised to another."

"Really?" He laughed again. "What a coincidence—so am I. She's the daughter of a wealthy merchant. Face like a malcontent camel's, but she does come with a rather attractive dowry."

"But...but I thought...I'd hoped..."

Jonas propped himself up on one elbow and looked down at her, his face creased with concern. "You and me? Together? I'm sorry, Raisa—I thought you understood..." His mouth opened and closed a few times, his words seemingly clotted in his throat. "Oh, dear," he said finally. "You're not some kind of simpleton, are you? Is that why they keep you locked away?"

Raisa sat up and drew away from him angrily. "Of course not," she said.

"Look," he said, palms raised in a conciliatory gesture, "I didn't mean to offend, but...well, a little romp in the garden is one thing, but stealing you away from the Sisters? That would make me the simpleton."

Abruptly, he got to his feet and extended his hand to help Raisa up to stand alongside him on shaky legs. "It's been lovely, really it has, but we could be discovered at any moment." He pressed his lips to her cheek in a chaste mockery of his earlier lustful kisses. "Be well, Raisa," he said, and she thought she detected a note of pity in his voice. Then he was off, scaling the wall and fleeing to freedom.

She stared at the spot on the wall where, until a few moments ago, the rope had dangled. It was not too late for her to run away; certainly, it would be more difficult to go alone, and she could not take the same route that Jonas had followed. She could go now, under cover of darkness—simply take a second set of keys from the sleeping guard and leave through the main entrance. Or she could take her time and plan, just as she had done to smuggle Jonas in and meet with him undetected.

But where would she go? What would she do?

It did not matter; anything would be better than facing the condemnation of the Sisterhood. The ritual...in truth, she did not know exactly what the ritual entailed, nor what the precise outcome would be. She suspected that even the Sisters did not know for sure, basing their calculations as they did on ancient, crumbling and incomplete texts. For all she knew, it would not work whether she were pure or not, and all her years of obedience and servitude would have been for nothing.

She hugged herself against the sudden night chill. Sleep would not come easily for her that night, nor for many nights to come, she expected.

Raisa could not leave without saying goodbye to the Mandragora. She trembled with apprehension at the world beyond the wall as she approached the tree, a meagre sack of purloined supplies slung over one shoulder. She touched her fingertips to her lips then pressed them to the trunk.

"Raisa…"

At first she thought it was just the whisper of the breeze in the Mandragora's leaves, but there was no breeze; the night was still. She froze and listened attentively. Could it be Jonas, returning to the wall after a change of heart?

"Raisa…"

The leaves on the Mandragora's branches rustled. They looked to be reaching toward her, as if to enfold her.

"I love you, Raisa."

"I forgive you, Raisa."

The voice was not so much carried on the air as whispered directly into her brain.

"You belong here, with me. Forget that other. Join with me at our appointed time, and no one will ever come between us again."

She looked from the tree to the wall to the courtyard door and back to the tree.

Where would she go? What would she do?

The Mandragora spoke to her, meaningless sounds of comfort and mercy. Overwhelmed, she pressed her face to its bark and wept.

Raisa was sure that her betrayal was plain on her face for all to see, but as the weeks passed and nobody paid her any more or less attention than usual, she dared to believe that it had gone undiscovered. The Mandragora did not speak to her again, and she began to wonder if, in her heightened state of distress, she had imagined it all. Nevertheless, she attended to it with exaggerated care, and when nobody was looking, leaned against it and whispered words of contrition into its branches. Imagined or not, the Mandragora had been right; her place was here, for no other reason than that she had nowhere else to go.

Then one morning, she was summoned to the chambers of Abbess Dorota. With her heart pounding, she made her way along the corridors, flanked by two stony-faced Sisters. Upon arrival, the Abbess's withered, impassive face gave Raisa no clue as to the purpose of the summons. An unfamiliar sister stood at Dorota's right shoulder. The new sister appeared only a few years older than Raisa, yet wore the habit of one fully professed. She returned Raisa's stare with an open and friendly expression that was most un-Sisterly. Raisa took the seat indicated by Dorota and fought to maintain an outer calm.

"It is almost time, Raisa," Dorota said. "In five days, a century of preparation in accordance with the ancient texts will come to fruition." She leaned over her desk, her eyes gleaming with fervour. "All that remains is to deliver your final lesson to prepare you for your wedding. This is Sister Gredel. She will assist you." The two Sisters exchanged a look that left Raisa puzzled.

"Until your bonding," Dorota continued, "you must fast and take twice-daily purification baths." She rose and tottered around her desk to envelop Raisa in a surprisingly powerful hug, a move that unnerved Raisa as she had never seen Dorota leave the comfort of her chair, let alone touch anyone.

"May the Spirit fill you," Dorota whispered. With that, and a final nod to Gredel, Raisa was dismissed.

It was not until the third day of her fast that Gredel called Raisa into the courtyard for her mysterious 'final lesson'. She stood swaying, dizzy from the lack of food and from the heady aroma of the herbs that had been cast into her baths and that clung to her skin. Gredel carefully locked the courtyard door behind her, then unfastened her wimple to reveal a head of glorious, golden blonde hair. She shook out her locks with a satisfied sigh and turned her face up to the sun.

"I do so miss the feeling of the breeze in my hair," Gredel said. "I owe my life to the Sisterhood, but some days I feel like I merely swapped one prison for another." Smiling, she shook her head at Raisa's bemused stare and took Raisa's hand, leading her to stand in front of the Mandragora.

"I used to be a child-whore," Gredel said. The pronouncement was so shocking, and delivered in such a matter-of-fact way, that Raisa thought at first that she had misheard. The notorious child-whores of the city were often the subject of playground gossip at the convent school; although she was excluded from the conversations, she listened as pruriently as the other girls.

"I was good at it, too," Gredel continued. "I was almost at the age that you are now, and nearing the end of my usefulness, when the Sisters rescued me. As you can appreciate, with a history as besmirched as mine, I was very, very fortunate to be admitted into the order. The Abbess is truly a visionary to have recognized my value." Her hand was still entwined in Raisa's, and she gave it a friendly squeeze. "My past, the Sisterhood, all of it was for a greater purpose. I exist only to be here, now, to show you what you must do."

She gestured with her free hand. "I cannot touch it. If you would part the leaves, just there…" Remembering the earlier warnings she had received against touching this part of the Mandragora, Raisa hesitated at first, but under Gredel's steady gaze, she bent to obey. The leafy growth at the top of its 'legs' was dense and luxuriant, and it took some minutes for her to fully expose what lay beneath.

The tubular protrusion that grew out at an angle from the trunk was smooth and thick and a slightly paler colour than the rest. Raisa stroked it tentatively with a forefinger. It was warm to the touch; in fact, it felt almost as if it were alive, as if it were a thing of blood and muscle, not wood and sap. Raisa turned her head at

Gredel's sharp intake of breath.

"Yes, good." Gredel nodded. "All is as it should be. Now cover it back up—no sense in scaring the acolytes, is there?" She helped Raisa to stand. "Now listen carefully," she said, staring intently into Raisa's eyes. "You must take that inside you."

"Inside me?" Raisa said. She knew, of course she knew, for she had recognised in the Mandragora's growth that same thing that Jonas had forced between her legs. But still, the thought of doing that with a tree…

Gredel took hold of Raisa's skirts and gathered them up in her fist, then took Raisa's hand and drew it down between Raisa's legs.

"Here," Gredel said soothingly, as if speaking to a frightened animal. She guided Raisa's middle finger into her vagina. "The herbs you have been bathing in will have helped to make your maidenhead supple, so there should be little pain." She moved Raisa's finger, out then in again. "There now, that's not so bad, is it? Just imagine this, only bigger…" She slipped Raisa's forefinger in next to her middle finger.

Gredel kept talking, coaxing, her breath warm and moist against Raisa's ear, her words jumbling into nonsense as Raisa moved her hand of her own volition, faster and faster, her own breath coming fast and shallow, her gaze never leaving the Mandragora.

The morning of her wedding dawned dull and overcast. Raisa lay listlessly in her cell for most of the day. As night approached, she allowed the Sisters to bathe her, to comb her hair and to dress her in a simple, white robe. She felt inanimate, unable to feel even the basest of emotions, like a giant living doll.

Or like her groom-to-be.

They led her into the courtyard, where the entire Sisterhood stood in a circle against the walls. The way they surrounded her, trapped her anew with their still and silent bodies, brought to mind an inquisition rather than a celebration. The flickering torchlight and the shadows cast by their hoods obscured their faces; Raisa could only imagine their expressions, malicious and accusatory. Gredel took her gently by one elbow and another, younger Sister took her by the other. They turned her around and slipped her robe off her shoulders to leave her standing naked before the Mandragora.

Raisa was only dimly aware of Dorota's thin, reedy voice raised in a chant. Gredel put a slight pressure on her arm and she took a step closer to the tree. Then another. She parted the leaves covering the protrusion, flinching a little at the muted gasp from some of the Sisters.

"Raisa," Gredel murmured, kindly yet insistent. "It is time." Gredel had already talked her through the mechanics of the act; with a deep, shuddering breath, and physically supported by the two Sisters on either side of her, she placed her hands on the Mandragora's branches, rose on tiptoe, and gently, carefully, lowered herself down onto the phallus.

"Raisa..."

The chanting grew louder as it was taken up by the rest of the Sisterhood, but it could not drown out that familiar, insistent voice, spoken only for her. Aided by the women at her sides, she slid slowly up and down on the phallus in time to the rise and fall of the chant.

"Raisa...I have waited so long for you, Raisa..."

Her nipples, teased erect by the chill evening air, brushed against the Mandragora's bark, sending a frisson of pleasure to her loins. The branches bent as if under a great weight, and she felt the tickle of twigs and leaves against her back. She wrapped her arms around the trunk and hugged it tightly.

Her aides continued to move her up and down, up and down, her movement hampered by her tight embrace. An exquisite tension spread throughout her body, and she shrugged off her attendants, her movements becoming small, rapid and instinctual. She wept tears of relief, of love, of absolution, of mounting, blind ecstasy.

...never come between us again...

The chanting faltered as the first cries of alarm sounded from the nearest Sisters.

"What's happening?"

"Something is wrong!"

"Stop her! She's going to…"

It was becoming harder and harder for Raisa to move. She glanced down to see the skin on her torso catch on the bark and somehow stretch as she tried to pull away from the Mandragora. It hurt, unbearably so. *Don't fight it, then,* some part of her said, and she listened, tightening her grip on the trunk and pressing as much of her body into the tree as possible.

An extraordinary sensation flooded her senses (*"…we are one…"*) as she convulsed with pure, undiluted pleasure (*"…never come between us…"*). Human hands tugged futilely at her, their touch on her skin muted by the eternal moment of unity in which she was suspended. A keening sound—Dorota, wailing, her life's work obliterated—penetrated Raisa's eardrums; she tried to raise her hands to cover her ears, but they were stuck fast, sunken into the wood (*flesh*) of the Mandragora. And soon enough, it did not matter, as the noises became at first muffled then non-existent, as if she were lowering her head into deep water.

Her heartbeat slowed, almost stopped, as the blood in her veins gave way to sap; from deep within her tree-spouse's core she felt an answering beat throb in time with hers. Her skin (*bark?*) tingled as new leafy growth began to sprout. It felt good, it felt right, no matter what the Sisters had feared; with a final sigh, Raisa exhaled the last vestige of her human self.

We are one.

Ugly

"**Y**ou'll want to have that removed," the doctor said. "Get it sent away for testing."

"What?" Janine's hand fluttered to her face and hovered over the small lump on the side of her nose. The lump had been there for at least two decades, most of her adult life, so the suggestion that it might be malignant shook her. *What am I going to tell Tim? The kids?* The last thing she wanted to do was alarm her family.

The doctor leaned forward to examine it more closely, his expression a curious blend of aversion and avarice. "Don't worry," he said, "it's my specialty."

Strange that no other doctor had been concerned by it before now. She suppressed the notion—the doctor was right, doctors were always right, it must be cut off, and quickly.

The doctor leaned back in his chair. "Now, what was it you wanted to see me about?"

"Umm...my back..."

He came out from behind his desk, asked her to swing one leg then the other, and perfunctorily probed the muscles of her lower back. "It's nothing," he said, evidently bored with her already. "Just a muscle strain. Go home. Take a couple of Panadol. Use a heat pack. Sleep on a thin mattress on the floor for a week or so." He held his thumb and forefinger apart, barely wide enough to accommodate a thick sheet of cardboard, to indicate the required dimension. "It will come right soon. Now, make sure you make an appointment with reception on your way out for that excision."

She needn't have worried about her family's reaction; they barely registered what she said when she recounted her doctor's visit, talking over her at the dinner table like they always did, and for once she was glad of it.

"Will you come with me to the appointment?" she asked her husband Tim later, and was instantly annoyed with herself for her plaintiveness. Tim rolled his eyes and huffed.

"Surely you can handle this by yourself," he said. "You know how busy I am at work. And it's not as if you're going under a general anaesthetic, or won't be able to drive afterwards or anything like that. It's just your face."

It's just your face. If that didn't put it in perspective, nothing would. Yet the lump, barely half a centimetre across and nestled in the curve between nose and cheek, took on elephantine proportions in Janine's mind over the week leading up to the procedure. Never mind the medical implications; it had been the first thing the doctor had noticed about her when she walked in the room, and she had to wonder—was it really that prominent? That offensive? How many other people in her lifetime had looked at the growth on her face and been repelled, but lacked the license conferred by a medical degree to mention it? She kept her head low, let her hair fall over her face like a curtain and stayed even quieter than usual. She could not decide whether she should be mortified for walking around blindly inflicting this grotesquery on others for so long, or whether her shame should be directed at her new, absurd level of vanity.

On arrival for her appointment, the doctor led her into a small treatment room, where he had her lie on her side on a bed. He snipped a small piece from the centre of a large, white cloth and covered her head with it, leaving only the growth exposed. Janine felt invisible beneath the sheet. She closed her eyes and breathed shallowly like a small, timid animal hiding in forest undergrowth. The doctor's voice came to her slightly muffled. It sounded almost as if he were talking to himself.

"I'll have to put in a stitch or two…it's in an awkward place."

Stitches? He never said anything about stitches before. Then… *Of course there'll be stitches, you fool. Where there are scalpels, there are stitches. And where there are stitches, there will be a scar.* It seemed like she was just swapping one facial disfigurement for another.

The needle for the local anaesthetic pricked at first, then stung, then burned. Janine whimpered beneath the sheet, the moment expanding to take an eternity before the doctor withdrew the needle. Something trickled down the side of her face, and the doctor fumbled at the side of the sheet to pass her some tissues.

Blood.

"Can you feel this?" the doctor said.

"No."

"What about this?"

"No."

Instruments clinked against a metal tray. More blood ran down her face. There was a distant tugging sensation, then he was stitching her wound. One of the stitches entered her skin outside the anaesthetised area, making her yelp; it felt as if it were halfway across her cheek.

The doctor pressed a couple of adhesive strips over the wound, then lifted the sheet, leaving her to push herself unsteadily to a sitting position.

"There it is," he said, indicating with a flourish towards a kidney bowl on the stand next to them. Janine peered into the bowl.

"Ew." Detached from her face, the bloodied mass of fatty tissue looked much bigger.

"Isn't it, though?" the doctor said triumphantly.

"So when should I expect the results of the test?"

The doctor looked surprised for a moment. "Oh, I don't know," he said, waving a hand dismissively. "It's probably just a wart. The test is a formality. Insurance wouldn't cover it if they thought we'd removed it for purely cosmetic reasons."

And there it is.

"Come back in a couple of days and I'll change your dressing."

The adhesive strips over the wound didn't quite cover the stitches, the tail end of which stuck out like the coarse black leg of some oversized insect. Reactions ranged from pointed avoidance of mentioning the obvious from adults to innocently tactless questions from children. Her own children were blunt.

"You should have just said no," her nine-year-old said. "You didn't need to have it cut off." Her pronouncement made, she flounced off to her room. All three of her children were like that— strong-minded, strong-willed and rock-solid sure of themselves and their place in the world. Janine stared after her daughter, mute with bewilderment and love, and wondered how her own diffident genes could have ever contributed to her children's creation.

The wound itched far more than Janine had anticipated so soon after the procedure. Her skin beneath the dressing felt hot and tight, and she wondered if it were getting infected. She didn't mention it to the doctor, sure that he would soon diagnose it if it was true, and she wasn't entirely surprised when he peeled back the dressing and paused.

"Oh," he said with a soft exhalation of breath, sounding almost as if someone had punched him in the stomach. He took up a cotton swab, moistened it with warm water and dabbed at Janine's face. She watched his expression intently, saw it ripen from mild concern to confusion with an edge of panic, and her own innards tightened in response.

"It almost looks as if it's growing back..." he murmured. Then he straightened and turned away, busying himself with something on the counter behind him. When he turned back, he was armed with a fresh dressing and an impassive expression.

"It's probably just swelling. Not all that uncommon. Make another appointment to have the stitches removed. I'm sure it will have settled down by then."

It did not 'settle down' as promised. Whatever was sprouting beneath the dressing, it was not the same as before. It expanded quickly, absorbing the stitches and pushing the dressing up and away until it clung precariously to the bulge of flesh by one stubborn little patch of adhesive. Finally, Janine ripped off the dressing and laid the growth bare. Within days it had grown to cover half of her right cheek. It threatened to extend over her right eye at its upper edge and the corner of her mouth at the lower edge. There was no longer any pretence of ignorance amongst her work colleagues; she deflected glances of distaste and abhorrence in the staffroom, the sphere of exclusion expanding with the unsightly growth until she commanded an eight-seater table to herself.

They fear me. Once that idea would have distressed her, but now she felt oddly smug, for lurking beneath the surface of that concept was another, more compelling one; *they notice me.* She squatted, a grinning gargoyle, in her little domain until her boss sent her home to 'recover'.

"Jesus, Janine!" an appalled Tim said. "When are you going back to the doctor? That's just not right!"

"I'm not going back to him," she said. "He's a fucking quack."

Janine never swore, yet seeing Tim recoil at the expletive made her wonder why not; the word had weight in her mouth and impact when she expelled it. Tim took a step back, then another, pausing to address her from the doorway.

"You'd better go see *some* doctor," he said. "You're starting to scare the kids."

The growth was smooth and pink, its greasy surface marred only by a couple of enlarged pores from which coarse, dark hairs sprouted. It had spread further—now it covered her right eye, crept across her scalp like a cowl, and descended down the front of her right shoulder, extending fleshy tendrils towards her nipple. So used to being all but invisible, she took perverse pleasure in displaying her deformity, venturing out to the local shopping plaza and observing passers-by flinch or turn away in ill-concealed horror. But driving had become difficult since her right arm had fused to her side, so she contented herself with staring in the mirror for hours on end.

Tim came into the bedroom, brimming with fake solicitude. He reached out tentatively to touch her, taking care not to come in contact with the growth. Beyond the closed door, the children could be heard shuffling and whispering, too scared to enter, too curious to stay away.

"Janine, sweetheart," he said. "I know you didn't want to go back to see your regular doctor, so I've called a skin specialist. I described your...problem...and he agrees, you need to see him urgently. We managed to get you an appointment for tomorrow morning."

She turned her good eye upon him and he blanched under the heat of her glare.

"Right then, love," he stammered. "I'll leave you to rest."

She returned her gaze to the mirror. All her life, she'd thought that beauty made the world go round, but now she was finding power in ugliness.

She could not have moved even if she wanted to; overnight, the growth had spread to completely cover her from head to knee. It tickled the tops of her shins, its cells replicating at an astonishing rate. A little light penetrated her cocoon, diffuse and flushed pink, occasionally cast over with shadow as someone walked past. External sounds were as muffled as a heartbeat, whereas her own heartbeat pulsed with an eerie clarity. A high-pitched tone penetrated. It was probably one of her children crying, but she observed it with detachment. Someone...no, several someones took hold of her and lifted her, then there was a slight pressure, presumably from straps securing her to a hospital gurney. She was swaddled, and swaddled again, and she revelled in the nurturing closeness; it was as if she had grown a womb about herself.

She sensed gentle, rhythmic movement, and it lulled her into a near-hypnotic state. She slept, and daydreamed, and slept again, reduced to little more than dim sensation and unfettered thought.

Janine awoke to pain. It started at her feet and sped upwards in an excruciating line of fire. She opened her mouth to scream and a sweet and sticky liquid rushed in to choke her. She coughed, spluttered, tried to spit it out, but her tongue…

What has happened to my tongue?

The pain intensified. She flailed, trying to escape it. There was a moist tearing sound, and the world rushed back in, assaulting her with light and noise and cold, hostile air. She unfolded, rising to a height she did not remember possessing. The massive sheath of skin that had been enclosing her body pooled in flaccid, bloody folds at her feet. A masked doctor cowered before her, his eyes moist with terror. Janine recognised those eyes…it was not a different doctor at all, but the same one that had cut up her face.

Tim had lied to her. The doctor had lied to her. Suddenly, it felt like the whole world had lied to her, and she longed with a delicious rage to retaliate and punish.

The doctor held a red-stained scalpel at arm's length and waved it about in an attempt to ward her off. The weapon looked pathetically tiny, and Janine laughed. The sound seemed to come from somewhere outside herself; it was the roar of a lion, the screech of nails down a blackboard, the voice of Hell on Earth. Another sound intruded, and she rounded on its source: a nurse screaming in a warbling, unpleasant timbre. Janine flung out an arm and neatly sliced open the nurse's throat with one black talon.

Talon?

Janine looked down in wonderment at what used to be her hands, ignoring the doctor gibbering in the corner. There were no mirrors in the room, so she dashed aside an array of surgical instruments on a gleaming metal tray and bent over the polished surface.

She smiled, and what was once her face contorted into new and interesting positions.

Ah, yes—ugliness becomes me.

Q is for Quackery

Marisa had given little thought towards what she would say to the man who killed her mother. He appeared to deeply value his privacy, not to mention his time, so most of her mental energy went towards finagling an appointment with him and raising the money to pay for it. She told herself that she only wanted to look upon him, to stare into his eyes and see what kind of monster would promise to heal a grievously ill woman, dissuade her from seeking conventional treatment, take her life savings and lead her to an agonising death.

But now she was face to face with him, the experience was nowhere near as cathartic as she had hoped. The address he'd given her was in an upper middle-class enclave of the city—affluent enough to suggest success, modest enough to avoid arrogance. Although he tried to imply otherwise, Marisa doubted that it was his home; the lounge in which she sat looked like that of a display house, decorated with meticulous good taste but devoid of the personal touches suggestive of actual habitation.

He introduced himself as Peter—not River or Merlin or whatever New Age name she'd imagined he might assume—and shook her hand with just the right degree of firmness. Also contrary to her preconceived notions, he was not dressed in a kaftan, beads and sandals, but wore dress trousers and a crisp, white collared shirt. He flashed a white-toothed smile which rendered his blandly handsome, middle-aged face indistinguishable from any number of stock photos designed to connote modern-day professionalism. Everything about him seemed calculated to project a specific image: assuring, competent, and unremarkable.

Marisa had to squash down the urge to spit in his face.

"How can I help you today?" Peter said, his expression radiating detached concern.

"I...well...my doctor doesn't know what's wrong with me." That much of Marisa's story she borrowed from her mother, whose pancreatic cancer was discovered almost too late for treatment. She stammered her way through a series of invented symptoms that could describe almost any illness—stomach pains, weight loss, headaches, fatigue—clutching at her body here and there. A vague notion of revenge began to crystallize in her mind, and she got involved in her fiction as she progressed.

Peter mimicked her gestures, his hands moving over his own body in a mirror image of hers, actions that were perhaps meant to signify sympathy and attentiveness but came across as almost mocking. Occasionally, he interrupted her tale to ask seemingly irrelevant questions. He sat up a little straighter to hear that she worked for a special effects company designing miniatures and prosthetics. "All those chemicals, the dyes and paints and synthetics, it's not good to be exposed to them on a daily basis. Not to mention what it must do to your psyche, having to channel your creativity in such restrictive ways." But most of his questions held an element of the absurd. Which direction did her bed face? What was her favourite colour? Was she fond of eating peanuts? They served to remind her that, despite his harmless façade, he was a dangerous quack who had to be stopped.

Eventually Marisa ran out of words. She sat in uncomfortable silence as Peter regarded her with an intent gaze. He moved off his seat and stood in an almost sexual pose before her, his groin close to her mouth, as he placed a hand on either side of her face and gently moved her head up and down and side to side.

"I'll need some hair samples," he said. "And nail clippings." He picked up her hand, examined her long, manicured fingernails, and gave a satisfied nod before letting it drop. "Your doctor won't have access to the kind of tests I need to run. And they're quite expensive, so you'll have to pay upfront. In cash." He quoted an exorbitant figure that sent Marisa clutching her purse a little tighter.

"But…you'll be able to heal me, right?" Her mother probably said much the same thing, and the thought made Marisa flush with barely contained fury.

Peter raised his hands in a non-committal gesture. "Well now, here's the thing—direct healing is only part of what I do. I'm also a facilitator. I teach people how to heal themselves, harnessing the power of their subconscious minds." He tapped his forehead. "If you truly want to be healed, then it will be so. But you have to want it badly enough."

Marisa fought to keep the derision from her voice. "That seems obvious, though…who wouldn't want to be well?"

"You'd be surprised," he said. "Some people come to me with deep-seated feelings of self-loathing, and they're not always receptive to the blessings of the Limitless Universe."

"And those people—do they get a refund?" This time, she could not entirely suppress the sarcasm. Peter looked at her for a long moment, his head tilted slightly to one side and a quizzical smile on his face, as if he were an inquisitive bird and she an unidentified object of dubious value.

"Those people," he said at last, putting an unusual stress on the first two words, "don't need money where they're headed."

For a split second, his smile turned feral. Marisa shuddered and lowered her head to busy herself in her purse as she took out his payment, telling herself that her tremors were induced by righteous anger and not bowel-chilling fear.

Safe in her own home later that night, Marisa let out a shaky laugh; damn it all if, after describing all those fictitious symptoms, she didn't really have a pounding headache.

Marisa's visit to the doctor had taken a decidedly ominous turn. She had planned to go for a routine check-up with her GP, obtain a clean bill of health, and use that to confront and discredit Peter when he came back with some false diagnosis that would no doubt be costly to treat. But the headache she'd come down with after her first visit to Peter had not abated. Over-the-counter pain relief was ineffective, and she'd been having dizzy spells, intermittent bouts of nausea and odd little black-out moments when she would come to with a shake to realize that she'd lost several seconds of awareness. The doctor had ordered an MRI scan, and now Marisa sat in her office and waited nervously for the results.

The doctor's expression was grave. "It's a brain tumour," she said bluntly. "No mistaking it…you can see the mass here." She pointed to the image of Marisa's brain and the large, whitish blob on the left-hand side. "We'll have to conduct further tests, but judging by the sudden onset of symptoms and the probable speed of its growth, I'd say it's malignant."

"And the treatment?"

The doctor sucked air in through her teeth. "An oncologist will be able to advise you further on that. Just looking at its position, I don't think surgery is going to be an option. Chemotherapy or radiotherapy perhaps…or, depending on its spread and aggressiveness, palliative care."

Palliative care. The doctor said it as if it were just another weapon in the medical profession's arsenal against disease, but Marisa knew what that really meant—*death sentence.* She was barely aware of the doctor's next words as she set up further tests and appointments. A small part of her said that she was just being paranoid, the paranoia perhaps even brought on by the tumour, but that voice was shouted down by a greater certainty: *Peter.* It couldn't be just coincidence. She had been fine before she went to see him, and now she could be dying. It was worse than she had originally thought; not only had he been exploiting vulnerable and desperate patients, but he had somehow been making them sick.

She drove to her next appointment with Peter in a rage-induced haze. She only had time to rap her knuckles on the door twice before he opened it, took one look at her, and said simply, "You're angry."

"Yes."

"You have a brain tumour—but you already knew that, didn't you?"

"Yes." Marisa did not trust herself to give more than terse answers. It would do no good to explode now, not when she needed to find a way to make him pay, make him hurt for what he had done to her, not to mention to her mother. Peter outlined a treatment regime that seemed to range from harmless to outlandish—organic vegetable juice breakfasts, coffee enemas, magnetic headbands, rearranging the furniture in her house for improved Feng Shui, a daily dose of a homeopathic remedy that bore a suspicious resemblance to plain tap water, and "absolutely no sugar"—to which Marisa paid scant attention.

"Now, Marisa, this anger..." He moved his hands vaguely about her head, as if her emotions were a mist he could dispel. "This is your greatest barrier to recovery. You must learn to let go. Whatever it is that is making you angry, you must make peace with it and move on."

Marisa smiled tightly and nodded. "Don't worry, Peter," she said. "Dealing with the source of my anger is my top priority."

Identifying Peter's car was easy; it was the only one parked in the street besides hers, all the other residents' vehicles being safely stowed in garages or having transported their owners to workplaces. Marisa's heart hammered in her chest as she crouched next to it, pretending to tie her shoelaces, and furtively attached the GPS tracking device under the wheel arch. It was a strangely exhilarating experience, this spying game, and she wondered if she had missed her calling. She got in her own car and drove a couple of blocks away, then settled in with her laptop to watch for any developments.

She didn't have long to wait. Less than fifteen minutes later, the little icon on her screen began to move across the map. She gave him a fair head start, then set off after him.

The tracking device led her to a well-kept cottage on the city fringes. Complete with a rambling wildflower garden and a white picket fence, it looked like the quintessential little old lady's home, not that of the middle-class professional Peter represented himself as. Perhaps he'd received the house as payment from one of his victims, Marisa thought, her knuckles whitening as she gripped the steering wheel.

She was writing down the address when a knock on the

passenger window startled her.

It was Peter, looking somehow younger now that he was out of his work environment, the dress trousers and shirt exchanged for jeans and a close-fitting black T-shirt. Even the sprinkle of grey in his hair had disappeared, although how that was possible in the relatively short period of time since she'd seen him last, Marisa didn't know. He beckoned to her to get out of the car.

She hadn't intended to confront him immediately, but the sight of him standing there so smug and healthy spurred her into action. She got out, slammed the car door with a fraction too much force, and strode towards him. She shoved him in the chest with stiff arms, sending him stumbling backwards.

"You did this to me!" she said, tapping the side of her head. "I don't know how, but I do know this—you're not getting away with it. Not anymore." As if on cue, her tumour asserted its presence; her vision swam, and she could have sworn she could smell sulphur and burnt toast. She swayed under the sensory onslaught, and Peter came forward to steady her with one hand under her elbow.

She fully expected him to deny the charges with feigned shock and incredulity. Instead, he leaned in close and whispered in her ear.

"You're only half right, sweetheart. Yes, I did this to you, but there's nothing you can do about it. After all, who is going to accept the word of a woman half-crazed with terminal brain cancer?" He released her and stepped back. "By the way, I'm not sorry about your mother. She was a lot like you—self-centred and aggressive, and completely deserving of everything she got."

"You...you knew all along who I was?"

"Oh, please. Give me some credit. I knew even before I laid eyes on you. I only agreed to meet you to see what you were going to do. And I have to say, I'm disappointed...so far you've been nothing but boringly predictable."

His dismissal shredded Marisa's last scrap of self-control. She flew at him then, hands contorted into claws, and scratched and tore at his face, his hair, his T-shirt, anything she could get her hands on. He reeled under the blows, but soon recovered, and stopped her with one well-placed punch that sent her sprawling onto her backside on the footpath and clutching a bleeding lip.

"I'll bury you!" she screamed through tears of pain and rage. "I'll fucking stab you in your sleep and burn your house down! I'll… I'll…"

Peter laughed. "That's it, Marisa, you make all those violent threats for the whole street to hear. If anything does happen to me, I'm sure that will make you the prime suspect." With that, he walked away.

The doctor had warned Marisa against driving, given the nature of her affliction, a caution that she had cavalierly ignored. It was nearing 10 pm when she stopped the car, the needle on the petrol gauge nudging empty, so she must have been driving around for hours with no awareness of where she had been. Her surprise lay not in the fact that her muscle memory had led her to work and not home where she had intended to go, but that she made it to any destination at all without ploughing into a lamppost.

Peter had been wrong about her work; it sustained and soothed her, the requirements and specifications of any given project giving her creativity direction and focus. She let herself into the studio and flicked on lights, breathing in the scents of clay, paint and silicone. With little conscious regard for what she was doing, she moved about the space, seeking only to find comfort and calm in a familiar activity. Somewhere around midnight she stopped in the middle of humming some half-forgotten pop tune, looked down, and realized what she had made.

It was a clay doll, about eight or nine inches long, clad only in a scrap of black cotton wrapped about its waist that Marisa must have torn from Peter's T-shirt and carried all the way here without noticing. The doll's features were a remarkable likeness of Peter, so accurately depicted that she half-expected the thing to get up and swagger across the table. It was easily the best work she had ever created.

Marisa raised her trembling hands before her eyes. Beneath her fingernails, drying clay intermingled with flecks of blood, although whether it was her own or Peter's, she could not say.

With a roar of hatred, Marisa attacked the doll, smashing and tearing and gouging with her modelling tools, until the effigy was nothing but an amorphous brown smear. The pressure in her head mounted exponentially, then there was a flash of brilliant white light, then…nothing.

The pain, the nausea, the tremors and the blurred vision…all of it was gone.

Marisa kept her appointment with the oncologist, who after analysing a battery of new tests, was forced to conclude that her original scan must have been swapped with someone else's.

"I'm so sorry," he said, "I don't know how it could have happened, but it appears that there is absolutely nothing wrong with you." It was an odd thing to apologize for, Marisa thought, but she smiled and nodded and shook his hand with genuine benevolence.

There was just one thing left to do now before she could consider herself fully healed, but it took her over a week to pluck up the courage for it. She loathed the idea that she could be afraid of Peter, but given that he had somehow inflicted a brain tumour on her that had just as miraculously disappeared, her fear was justified. Ultimately, though, curiosity won out.

It was a brilliant spring afternoon when Marisa pulled up outside Peter's cottage for a second time, yet the house seemed shabby and diminished, as if it sat under the shadow of its own little cloud. As she knocked on the door, the weight of her knuckles pushed it open.

"Hello?" she called into the gloom. She took a tentative step inside, and was answered with a faint groan. She followed the sound, and as it grew more distinct, so too did the stink of human filth: urine and sweat, faeces and vomit, and blood long since clotted. She found Peter —at least, she assumed it was Peter, for the skeletal creature in the bed bore little resemblance to the man she had last seen only a few weeks ago—alone in a room near the back of the house. He turned pain-filled eyes to her and opened a mouth full of rotting teeth to give her a ghastly parody of a smile.

"Come to gloat?" The words were uttered in a hoarse whisper and followed by a racking fit of coughing. Bloody spittle leaked from the corner of his mouth as he slumped back onto a filthy pillow.

"I don't know what you mean," she said. "I only came to try and get some answers."

Wide eyed, he stared at her. "You really don't know, do you?" She shook her head.

"Pity," he croaked. "If you gave the curse back to me by accident, then you have some real power. I could have trained you up. We could have made a formidable pair."

The stench wafting off him was phenomenal, yet Marisa came as close as she could stand. "I will never be like you," she said.

He made a gasping, hissing sound that Marisa realized was his dying attempt at laughter.

"If you want to keep on living, then you'll have to be."

Marisa knew the instant Peter died. It was like being hit with a sledgehammer—excruciating pain struck her entire body with breathtaking suddenness, literally sending her to her knees.

"Oh my God, Marisa, what is it? Are you OK?" her co-worker Gary said. He rushed around the workbench, oozing solicitude.

Arsehole, she thought through the fog of pain. Gary had a well-earned reputation as a sleaze; even now he was taking the opportunity to surreptitiously grope her breasts under the pretence of helping her up.

Marisa had been thinking, long and hard, about recent events. Peter had been less than forthcoming about the technicalities of his peculiar skill, but if she had surmised correctly, she knew what she needed to do. And she needed to do it quickly.

She clung tightly to Gary, wrapping her arms around his neck and hiding a grimace as she felt his semi-erection prod her. "I don't know what's come over me," she said in a breathy whisper. "I think I need to go home." Gary wore his hair longish, past his collar in the mistaken belief that it made him look sexy, and Marisa looped a few strands around one forefinger. Abruptly, she sagged in his arms, letting her full weight carry her back towards the floor. Gary was unprepared, and he yelped as she pulled out several long, dirty blonde hairs and concealed them in her palm.

After such a dramatic exit, she dared not return to the studio that evening, even if she had been able to push through the pain and ever-increasing weakness. She made do at home with whatever materials she could find, and when she was finished, she had to admit that the little Gary doll was a pretty good replica under the circumstances. She took a few moments to admire her handiwork before affixing the strands of hair to the doll's head.

The energy was the key now, she felt. The animosity and viciousness with which she destroyed the doll was not only for Gary, but for Peter, for her doctors who were next to useless, for her mother for dragging her into this mess, for the cop who gave her a speeding ticket last week and for her neighbour who played drum and bass at full volume at 2 o'clock in the morning. It was for the murderers and the rapists, the puppy kickers and the crooked politicians, for the whole fucking world and every shitty person in it.

When it was done, she slept the pain-free sleep of the righteous and whole.

Nine weeks later, the studio closed for a day while everyone attended Gary's funeral. Marisa was not in attendance; she had resigned shortly after her "turn," ostensibly citing health reasons, which was in a way true; she'd become self-employed, building up a discreet and lucrative business as an alternative healer.

Her latest client was a grey-faced and nervous creature who called herself Fifi—a ridiculous name for a grown woman, Marisa decided. Fifi was in her early thirties according to the form she had completed, but looked much older. Marisa tuned out as Fifi described her extensive list of symptoms. Instead she focussed intently on taking in her features—the line of her nose, the angle of her jaw, the shape of her eyes, the peculiarities of her hairline. Marisa's hands twitched in her lap, eager to get to work on the sculpture. Peter's words came back to her—*if you truly want to be healed, then it will be so*—and she realized now what he meant. Many of her clients didn't really want to be well. They wanted the attention and sympathy that came with being sick, and the feeling of specialness and martyrdom that came with having an illness that was hard to diagnose. The realization only increased her contempt for them.

Her attention snapped back to the client, who sat looking at her expectantly.

"Do you think you can help me?" Fifi asked.

Marisa pretended to consider the question. "First, I'll need some samples from you—some nail clippings, and several strands of hair—for testing." She took a pair of nail scissors and a plastic bag from a small box on the table and handed them to Fifi. "I have to send the samples to Germany," she lied. "The tests are so cutting edge that your doctor probably doesn't even know about them, and they'll tell me things that conventional medicine can't." Fifi nodded, apparently reassured.

"But I must emphasize," Marisa went on, taking Fifi's hand and gazing into her eyes with what she hoped was an earnest expression, "that whatever your ailment, you will only recover if you truly want to. My role is mainly to guide you in your personal journey of self-healing."

Fifi frowned. "But of course I want to recover. Who wouldn't?"

Marisa sat back and smiled. "Oh, you'd be surprised…"

The Accession of Stinky

"**S**omething followed me home again." Alicia slung her school bag in the corner of the room and headed straight for the fridge.

It had been a long time since something had followed her home. Now that Alicia was nearing seventeen, Diane thought that she'd stopped bringing home strays.

"Where is it?" Diane asked.

Alicia held a drumstick in one hand and an apple in the other. She waved the drumstick like a negligent conductor. "Outside the front door."

Diane sighed. She was the one who fed and fussed over the things, overcompensating for her daughter's indifference to the besotted creatures. She always wanted to keep them, but her husband would never allow them in the house. Anyway, they were always gone by morning, often without a trace, but occasionally leaving little mementoes of fur or feathers or scales. The last one had left a large puddle of viscous black goo on the doorstep, as if it had dissolved there in the night.

She opened the door.

"Oh, it's so...ew."

Even with her hyperactive mothering instinct, Diane wasn't tempted to keep this one.

It was bigger than the others, about the size of a Labrador. Several large yellowing fangs jutted up from its lower jaw. Its eyes were set wide on either side of a squat skull, and they seemed to roll independently of each other in rheumy sockets. Large black warty bumps covered its dun-coloured hide. As it caught sight of Alicia coming up behind her, it began to drool with excitement, its breath labouring through flattened nostrils. Its paddle-like tail thumped vigorously, sending up dust clouds from the door mat.

"It's lovely, isn't it?" said Alicia sarcastically. "I think I'm going to call him Stinky." Alicia crouched and offered the creature the drumstick. It extruded a long slimy tongue and used it like a prehensile limb to take it from her. Shards of bone fell like crumbs from either side of its mouth as it ate.

"You call all of them Stinky."

But Alicia was already walking away.

"**W**hat the fuck is that thing guarding the front door? It wouldn't let me in." Tim tracked mud in from the back yard across Diane's freshly mopped kitchen floor. He grabbed a beer from the fridge and stood at the kitchen bench taking long pulls from the bottle.

"Just something that followed Alicia home from school." Diane refrained from stating the obvious—he was late again, and his dinner was slowly cooling on the table.

"You're still bringing home strays? Thought you'd stopped all that shit."

Alicia shrugged. Tim slid into his seat and looked sideways at his daughter as he loaded his plate from the serving dishes in the centre of the table.

"And while we're on the subject of growing up, don't you think it's about time you stopped wearing pigtails? It was cute when you were five. Now it's just..." He trailed off, looking to Diane for back-up. "You know what I mean, don't you?"

They were used to Tim's ritual; he had to spend the first ten minutes or so after returning home from work complaining and criticizing before he could settle into the role of loving husband and father. Alicia slowly batted her lashes at her father, once, twice, her face a serene mask.

Diane studied her daughter. As was the fashion amongst Alicia's peers, she wore her school uniform cut perilously short, the hem barely covering her butt. Diane had been jokingly calling her the Perpetual Motion Machine since she was a baby; right now she was jiggling one long, lean, tanned leg under the table. Her breasts strained against the fabric of her blouse, and no wonder, Diane thought—it was last season's. Diane made a mental note to buy her the next size up.

She looks like a stripper in a naughty school girl costume, Diane thought. She pushed the image aside. "How was your day?" she said to Tim, pointedly changing the subject.

He grunted and pointed towards the front door. "Just make sure you get rid of that thing tomorrow."

Diane studied herself naked in the mirror. Had she been as gorgeous as Alicia when she was seventeen? She had a feeling that she had, but looking at her sagging chin, her crow's feet and frown lines, her flabby belly and flaccid breasts, it was hard to remember. I look like I'm melting, she thought, and suppressed a hysterical giggle.

Some days she felt like Sleeping Beauty's stepmother, seething with jealousy whilst her child grew more beautiful every day. On other days, she was the victim, and Alicia the villain, sucking her life force from her to augment her own and leaving her mother a dried-up husk. Perhaps I should dig out some old photos, she thought. Her memories could be playing tricks on her. If she were to look back on her youth and find that she had in fact been plain, it would make her aging easier to bear; she need not mourn the loss of something she never had.

Stinky was still there in the morning. It appeared to have grown a little overnight. And, if such a thing were possible, it had become even uglier. Alicia absently scratched it behind one of its scabby ears as she left for school. Tim exited via the back door. He refrained from commenting on it when he returned that night, focusing instead on the blown light bulb in the hallway and the dirtiness of the kitchen floor. The week came and went, and it appeared that Stinky had succeeded where all the others had failed; through a combination of its persistence and everyone else's apathy, it had inveigled its way into the family.

Diane didn't know how it was getting so big. She hadn't seen anyone in the household feed it, and there was no conspicuous plundering of groceries to suggest that Alicia was sneaking it food. And she didn't think it was getting nourishment elsewhere either; it spent all its time squatting like a gargoyle on their doorstep. It moved only to let Alicia or Diane through, or to defecate in a corner of the garden. Alicia was spending a little time with it now, stopping after school for a few minutes to pet it and talk to it while it salivated happily on her shoes. Maybe that's all the nourishment it needs, Diane thought. Or, more likely, it was sneaking out to hunt while they slept. She imagined it loping down the road, its jaws closing on someone's pet cat, the flying fur and agonised squeal as it dismembered its victim, and her stomach turned.

Diane woke with a start. She could have sworn she'd heard a noise. She shuffled through the dark to the kitchen to get a glass of water. Something tugged at her awareness, and she crossed to the front lounge to draw back a corner of a curtain and peer out.

Stinky stood with its paws on the top of the gate. Its head was thrown back, its throat muscles working in a silent howl. It must have been calling at frequency beyond the range of human hearing; although she could not hear it, she could feel it, vibrating in her bones. Her heart raced, her mouth flooded with saliva, the hair on the back of her neck stood erect, and so did her nipples, grazing uncomfortably against her nightgown. She went back to bed and lay awake for what seemed like hours. When she finally fell asleep, she dreamt of King Stinky summoning his army. She dreamt that she watched from the top of a tall medieval tower as hundreds of lesser Stinkys ran through suburban streets to congregate at her door. What do they want? her subconscious whispered. Perhaps if she were to add her howl to King Stinky's, they could find the strength to break down the door, and they could be upon her in minutes. The thought filled her with a disconcerting mixture of dread and arousal.

Stinky's siren song must have affected Alicia as well. Either that, or she was coming down with something. She looked pale and felt feverish when Diane pressed the back of her hand to her forehead.

"Go back to bed," Diane said. "I've got to go to work today, but you can ring me if you really need me."

Even Stinky looked worn out. It dozed on the doorstep and barely looked up when Diane walked past it on her way out. It had become almost as big as a lioness, so it was forced to sprawl in an awkward position with its head and front paws on the door mat, its body on the stairs and its back paws scraping the path.

Lucky bastard, thought Diane. I wish I had the luxury of sleeping it off. Several cups of coffee did nothing to clear the cobwebs from her head. She convinced herself that Alicia needed looking after and left work two hours early. She stopped at the supermarket on the way home, wandered the aisles aimlessly, and ended up leaving with just a king size block of chocolate and a magazine. Sod it, she thought, Tim can pick up takeaway on the way home.

She was dimly aware that something had changed when she got home, but it wasn't until she was three paces inside the house that she realised what it was. Stinky was not on the doorstep. A quick check out the back confirmed that it wasn't there either. There were sounds coming from Alicia's bedroom, muffled through the not-quite-closed door. Diane heard a feminine voice, giggling, and an unidentifiable noise that was like a hybrid purr-growl-slurp. She lingered at the door, alarm mounting, as the giggles gave way to the unmistakable sound of a woman approaching orgasm.

Diane slowly pushed the door open with her fingertips and took a step into the room. Alicia lay naked on her bed, her eyes squeezed shut, oblivious to her mother's presence. Stinky crouched between her spread-eagled legs, its agile tongue working furiously between them. Alicia arched her back and spasmed with one last breathless scream, then collapsed back onto the bed. Stinky crept up to nuzzle first one nipple, then the other, and came to rest with its full body length pressed against hers. Alicia caressed its bumpy head.

"I love you, Stinky," she whispered. With her lungs compressed under Stinky's weight, she sounded how Diane imagined Stinky would talk, if it could.

Diane's mouth worked soundlessly. That's not love, she wanted to shout, that's...

Stinky's eyes rolled in her direction, its mouth open wide as if it were grinning at her.

Go on, it seemed to say, why don't you tell her what it really is.

The Changing Tree

Sten and his class tumbled into the town square in a flurry of flailing limbs. It was the start of Izbirith week, and seven blessed days of leave stretched out before them. Seven days to run, to climb, to hunt, to fish, to fight… Filled with exuberance, he shoved his friend Liath in the shoulder. Liath shoved back, and they grappled for a moment before falling to the ground. Liath was easily the stronger of the two, but Sten could rely on Liath to allow him to win at least half of the time; it was one of the many reasons why Liath was his best friend. Sten sat astride Liath's back and tightened his grip with his thighs as Liath writhed beneath him.

"Let me up, you stinking scrap of dog dung," Liath said, his voice muffled as Sten rubbed his face into the dirt.

A strong scent of lavender wafted towards Sten. He scrambled to his feet, offering a dusty hand to Liath and hauling him up. They bowed their heads as a trio of priestesses walked past. Their pale blue robes concealed all but their faces. Whenever Sten saw them, he got the disconcerting impression that they were fallen pieces of sky floating on the surface of the earth. He waited until the priestesses had passed out of sight behind the town hall before renewing his assault on Liath.

Liath pushed him away with one hand and swept a lock of dark hair out of his eyes with the other. He stood looking towards the Changing House on the hill.

"It'll be Changing Day soon," he said. "Who do you think will be chosen?"

Sten groaned. Trust Liath to remind of him of what Izbirith week was really about. Some of the other boys gathered closer.

"I heard that the priestesses write each boys' name on a piece of parchment, put the pieces in a big pot, and draw them out one by one until they have the right number of names," said one.

"Naw, that's not right," said another. "I heard they pick the littlest, prettiest boys. That way they don't have to change so much."

"You're sure to be picked then, Sten," said Liath, wrapping his arm around Sten's neck and rubbing the top of Sten's head with his knuckles.

Sten pulled himself free. "Well, I heard that it really hurts. The priestesses make a potion from the fruit of the pesago tree, and it's like poison. It feels like your insides are being minced up with a big knife. And they make you drink it every day. That's why the chosen ones have to live in the Changing House until they've changed completely—so nobody can hear their screams."

The boys muttered nervously and huddled a little closer together. None of them knew for sure how it worked. The only certainty was that at the end of Izbirith, roughly half their number would be taken by the priestesses to the Changing House. And there they would stay out of sight until they emerged three years later, like butterflies from a cocoon, changed into women.

The town's three pesago trees stood in the centre of the temple courtyard, which was enclosed by a stone wall that towered over the boys' heads. Six white wolves patrolled the courtyard, further ensuring that only the priestesses could gain access to the trees. Sten and Liath teetered on their makeshift ladder and peered over the top of the wall. It was a time-honoured tradition; despite it being expressly forbidden, nearly every boy in town had done the same at one time or another, drawn by the dangerous allure of the wolves.

The wolves' snowy pelts glowed in the moonlight, their massive neck and shoulder muscles flexing as they paced the perimeter of the wall. Confronting the creatures' size for the first time, Sten caught his breath; had he been foolish enough to jump down on the wrong side of the wall, he would have found himself standing eye to eye with them. One wolf paused directly beneath them, sniffed the air and looked up, giving a low, uncertain growl. The boys ducked down out of sight.

"What stops them from attacking the priestesses?" Sten whispered.

Liath frowned. "I think it's something to do with their smell. The wolves are trained not to touch anything that smells like lavender. That, and—" he wrinkled his nose "—they have that woman smell."

Sten had no idea what a 'woman smell' was meant to be, but he nodded gravely anyway. They stood in comfortable silence, their backs pressed against the cool stone wall, breathing in the more reassuring odours of freshly cut pine and their own sweet-sour sweat.

"Liath...if one of us gets chosen, and the other doesn't, do you think we'll still be friends when the change is over?"

"Why wouldn't we be?" Liath jostled against him, already impatient to be off.

Sten hugged himself in the darkness. "I don't want to change," he whispered.

"We won't," Liath whispered back. "Not in any way that matters."

Then he gave Sten a shove that nearly unbalanced him off the ladder. "Anyway, no need to be such a sook, Sten. Anyone would think you'd changed into a woman already. C'mon—I'll give you a race. Last one home is a smelly priestess."

Sten studied his parents over the dinner table and tried to imagine them as children. It was easy to picture Father as a young boy. He would have been a lot like Liath—large, loud, always laughing and often in trouble. Sten's little brother Callum scrambled down from the table and Father scooped him up onto his lap, tickling him mercilessly under the armpits until Callum giggled himself breathless. Father joined in the laughter, his teeth flashing white against his thick black beard. Sten stroked his own hairless chin.

But Mother...? She sat still and distant, a small smile playing about her lips as her gaze slid over her family and away. It seemed like she was present only in body, her mind off exploring in some foreign land that was impassable to all but her. She rose from the table and began to clear dishes, humming quietly to herself. Father lifted a hand as if to caress her cheek, then dropped it, his own smile dimming for a moment as she passed him by.

"Men are the doers," a priestess would tell them in the temple on Sabbatday, "the makers, the builders, and sometimes, when need be, the destroyers. Women are the thinkers, the planners, the dreamers. Apart, they are weak, directionless, impotent." She would hold her hands wide apart, waggling her fingers, then lace them together to form a two-handed fist. "But mesh them together, and their disparate energies combine to create a powerful force. It is here that we mortals come closest to the Divine."

Contemplating his family, Sten shook his head. The priestesses must have that wrong, he thought. He didn't see any meshing going on around here, nor any evidence of the Divine, whatever that might look like. All he saw was two profoundly different people who seemed barely able to acknowledge each other's existence.

Later, when Mother came to his room to bid him goodnight, Sten asked, "Did you and Father like each other much when you were boys?"

She frowned, pausing for a long moment as if struggling to recall. "Why, yes," she said finally. "In fact, we were best friends." Her frown deepened, aging her suddenly. Then she shook herself a little, smiled, and bent to kiss on the forehead. "Now get to sleep. We've all got a big day tomorrow."

Tomorrow was Changing Day. No matter what happened, Sten vowed to himself, he would not let it affect his friendship with Liath. Never, ever, ever.

There were thirty twelve-year-old boys that year. They stood in a line in front of the temple altar with their immediate families clustered behind them. The rest of the town stood at their backs and spilled out the door. A priestess stood before them and recited each boy's name, gesturing either to her left or her right. The boys sent to her left were those chosen to undergo the change, and the priestess paused to allow those boys time to farewell their families. Some of the boys reacted stoically, some with tears, and some with barely restrained anger. One or two looked pleased about it, which puzzled Sten. The process seemed to be taking forever, and the press of bodies inside the temple made it uncomfortably hot. Sweat tickled his neck, and he resisted the urge to pull at his collar.

Finally, only he and Liath remained in front of the priestess. Sten grabbed Liath's hand, disregarding the sniggers from some of the other boys, and squeezed tightly. Liath squeezed back.

"Sten Stoutarms," said the priestess. She raised her arm and moved it to her right. Sagging with relief, Sten moved to join the other boys. His parents smiled and nodded, obviously as pleased as he was with the decision.

"Liath Truthsinger." The entire village seemed to hold its breath as the priestess lifted her hand, slowly, slowly, and with a gesture of welcome, moved it through a graceful arc.

To her left.

Liath bowed in acknowledgment, his face was an impassive mask. He turned to his family, stiffly embracing his father and mother. One of his older brothers made as if to punch him on the shoulder, pulling the punch at the last minute to send his fist barely brushing against Liath's body. The other brother looked down at his feet before pulling Liath into a bear hug.

Then his farewells were over. He joined the end of the queue of boys bound for the Changing House and, without a backward glance, followed the priestess from the temple. Sten stared at his retreating back.

Father tugged at his sleeve. "Sten. Let's go. It's over now. Time for the festival." The second part of Changing Day was due to begin, when the village would welcome back the women who had been selected as boys three years previously. Eager to escape the pressing heat, the crowd had dispersed rapidly, leaving Sten and his family to straggle at the rear. Sten swiped the back of his hand across his face, dashing away his tears.

"Don't worry about Liath," Mother whispered. "The change… it's not that bad. And she won't be alone."

Sten choked back a sob. "But I will be," he murmured, too low for anyone to hear.

The Changing House was easily the largest structure in the village, having to house up to one hundred boy-women at various stages of transformation. It was really a small network of buildings linked by internal walkways. There were two external doors at each end of the House, one through which the chosen ones entered at the beginning of their exile, and one through which they would exit at the end. A white wolf was tethered outside each door; whether their purpose was to keep intruders out or keep the House occupants in, Sten was not sure. He gave the wolves a wide berth as he crept around the walls searching for a likely location for the dormitories.

The windows were all barricaded with wooden slats that could be levered open a little to let in light and air. It was an unseasonably warm evening, and the susurrus of many sleepers could be heard through the open slats at the far end of the House. Sten crouched beneath one window and closed his hands over his mouth to imitate the soft, plaintive call of the sova bird. He called twice, paused for ten heartbeats, then called twice more. It was a code that only he and Liath knew, and he waited beneath the window for Liath's response. Hearing nothing, he moved to the next window.

Half way along the wall, the answering call came.

"Liath! Is that you?"

"Yes."

"Are you OK? What's it like in there? Have you drunk the pesago potion yet? Does it hurt?"

Liath cut off the flood of questions. "We're fine. The potion doesn't hurt, although the priestesses say it might later, when the changes start to happen. It's not like any of the stories we heard. I wish I could describe it to you, but I don't think you would understand."

Sten leaned against the building as if he could reach Liath

through the walls. "We're best friends. Of course I'll understand."

The reply, when it came, sounded distant. "I'm going now—I'm really tired. Be seeing you, Sten."

The next time Sten went to the Changing House, he called beneath every window, but received no reply.

H is mouth full of nails, Sten grunted as he bent to lift the horse's hoof. When Wardren the blacksmith had taken him on as an apprentice the year before, he had been unsure of his suitability to the trade. But he had soon found it fitted him well. He was a quick learner, and with the constant physical exertion, he soon built muscle on his lean frame. And the long hours left him with little time to daydream.

The mare leaned her weight on Sten, and he nudged her with his shoulder. "Nearly finished," he muttered reassuringly. He hammered the last nail into place and lowered her hoof.

Wardren's huge, soot-covered hand clapped him on the shoulder. "Good work, Sten. Why don't you go home early? The women Emerging from the Changing House tomorrow—they're your year, aren't they? You'll be wanting to scrub off some of that dirt so you can look your best for them." Wardren tipped him a huge wink.

Sten smiled uneasily back at Wardren as he untied his apron. There was some meaning behind Wardren's words that he was missing. It was only respectful that he present himself neatly at the festival, he supposed, but Liath had never cared before whether or not he was dirty.

Except it would not be Liath anymore, he remembered. She would have chosen a new name and would announce it to the town tomorrow. He looked down at his bulging biceps and blackened, calloused hands. Yes, he decided, he must clean himself up. It would be hard enough for her to recognise him as it was.

S ten fussed over his appearance longer than he should have, and ended up late for the Emerging festival. From his distant vantage point at the edge of the town square, the faces of the Emerged women on the stage were little more than smudges. As they each announced their new names, their voices were lost in the buzz of chatter around him. As soon as the naming ceremony was over, Sten pushed through the throng towards the small group of Emerged.

A hand touched lightly on his forearm. "Sten?"

The voice was soft and high-pitched, like a child's. Sten looked down to see a slender, dark haired young woman.

"It's me, Liath. Or should I say, Liana." The woman covered her mouth and looked down, then coyly returned her gaze to Sten's.

Sten gaped. The woman ran her fingers through her hair, just like the old Liath used to do when he was nervous. If he looked closely, he could see the ghost of his old friend in her eyes, and perhaps there was something familiar in the tilt of her head. Liath had always been the bigger of the two, but now Sten towered over her. It was as if he had gained all the bulk that she had lost, and then some. Yet there was something in the way she was looking at him that made him feel like a small boy all over again.

"I'm a blacksmith now," he blurted. "Well, almost. I've just entered the second year of my apprenticeship."

Liana trailed her hand down his arm to brush his fingers, sending a tiny shiver up his spine. The soot from the smith was deeply ingrained in the skin of his hands, and he had not been able to entirely scrub it away. "So I see," she murmured. She withdrew her hand and looked away over her shoulder, seeming to focus on something in the middle distance. He had seen that same dreamily distracted look on his mother's face many times.

"So...tell me all about the Changing House," Sten said, desperately trying to get her attention back. "It's been three years since we last spoke—I imagine you've got hundreds of stories saved up for me."

"Hmm...what?" Reluctantly, Liana returned her gaze to his. "Oh, no." She raised a finger to her lips. "Secret women's business," she said with a smile, then looked around her again. Her eyes lit up as she spotted someone in the crowd, then she stood on tiptoe.

Her lips brushed against his cheek, a butterfly's touch on his suddenly too-hot skin.

"Later—we'll talk."

Just as Liana was officially a woman today, Sten was officially a man. And being a man meant he was allowed to drink as much hard cider as he wanted. He poured his fourth cup and returned to his seat, sloshing half of it onto the ground on the way. The cider was starting to taste as bitter as his mood, but he swallowed it down anyway, his eyes never leaving Liana. She sat in a cluster of other young women, their heads almost touching as they whispered and giggled amongst themselves. Liana detached herself from the group to approach a man a few years older than her. Her hands flitted through the air as she touched his arm, his hand, his face. He bent to whisper something in her ear, and she pressed her body close against his for a moment, then drew away, her head thrown back in laughter.

Sten dashed the dregs of his cider on the ground and stalked away. He couldn't stand to watch any more. Three years he had waited for her return, and she could barely spare him five minutes of her time. If she hadn't been chosen, there would be no secrets between them, and they would still be friends. But that could not be undone. The divide between their different sexes could not be crossed.

Or could it…?

The changes wrought on Liath-now-Liana's body could not be reversed, this was true. But maybe he could change to become more like her. An idea formed in his befuddled mind, and he walked faster, intent on executing it before his resolve failed.

With all the priestesses and their acolytes attending the festival, the temple and attached living quarters were deserted. Sten blundered about for what seemed like half the night until he found what he was looking for—a laundry room, complete with several hampers of soiled robes. He scooped up an armful of azure fabric and breathed deeply, savouring the lavender scent. Although roomy enough, most of the robes were too short to adequately cover him, but eventually he found one that reached down to his ankles. It would have to do, he thought as he fumbled with the robe's fastenings.

Cider swirled unpleasantly in his stomach as he located the door that led out into the courtyard. It was locked, the key hanging high up on the wall. Some negligent acolyte had left the hooked staff needed to retrieve it leaning near the door. Sten's hands shook as he lifted the key down, and the key clattered on the stone floor, the sound echoing throughout the hallway. From beyond the door came a muted barking. Sten took several deep breaths to slow his racing heart. Then he unlocked the door and stepped outside.

The pesago trees stood less than fifty paces away. The wolves scarcely looked in his direction, except for one, which pricked up its ears and padded over to him. Sten tried to emulate a priestess's tread as he took a step towards the tree, then another, then another. The wolf butted its head affectionately against Sten's hip. Sten ignored it, his every muscle trembling in fear, and kept walking. The wolf tilted its head to one side quizzically, a gesture that Sten might have found amusing had his life not been at such great risk. It butted him again, more insistently this time, and pushed its head beneath his hand.

"Nice doggy," Sten whispered. The wolf kept pace with him as he fondled its ears and advanced with agonising slowness towards the tree. It licked his fingers, then stopped and backed up a few paces, sinking onto its haunches and giving a low growl. Five more pairs of lupine eyes turned in his direction.

Sten did not hesitate. He grabbed the hem of the robe, hitched it up around his thighs, and ran.

The wolves were fast, but Sten's terror lent him a momentary advantage. He leaped for the lowermost branch of the nearest tree, gripping it firmly and swinging his legs up out of the reach of the wolves' snapping jaws. One jumped up and sank its teeth into Sten's robe. For a precarious few seconds it hung on, dangling in mid-air, its weight threatening to pull Sten out of the tree. The robe ripped, the wolf tumbled to the ground with an undignified yelp, and Sten scrambled further up the tree to safety.

He leaned back against the trunk and drew in huge gulps of sweet, life affirming air. The wolves, aware that he was out of their reach for now, stalked about the base of the tree, growling in concert with their hackles raised.

Sten plucked a fruit from a branch. Shaped like a flattened apple, and with a glossy purple skin, it fit comfortably in the palm of his hand. It was heavier than it looked, and as he raised it to his lips, it almost felt as if it were resisting him. The wolves cowered beneath him, and one raised its muzzle to the sky and let out a mournful, bone-chilling howl.

Sten sunk his teeth into the fruit. It was all flavours, all at once, sweet and salty and fiery and bitter. He grabbed another fruit, and another, mashing them into his open mouth as fast as he could. He looked down, following the progress of several droplets of juice from his chin to the ground. They seemed to be falling impossibly slowly. He leaned towards them, and felt himself falling after them. He, too, moved through the air as slowly as sap oozing down a tree trunk. He had time to wonder if this was how Liana had felt all those years, drinking the priestesses' pesago potion, and he felt a fierce surge of empathy before he was blanketed in darkness.

Callum stood in the middle of the knot of boys and stared up at the priestess. You are privileged, they had told them, to be the first boys to be allowed into the courtyard, but he didn't feel that way at all. He didn't know which terrified him more, the wolves, the cold-eyed woman in her blue robes, or the prospect of seeing his brother again after so many years.

"My name is Liana," the priestess said. "You will be quite safe as long as you obey a few simple rules. Do not cross the threshold until I tell you it is safe to do so. Stay on the path, and do not attempt to touch the wolves. Is that clear?"

Thirty-three heads nodded in unison. Liana unlocked the door to the courtyard, stepped forward, and spoke a few words of command. As one, the wolves lowered themselves to the ground.

Liana beckoned the children forward. She took a deep breath, and Callum braced himself for a speech about sacred duties or trust in the Divine or some other lofty concept. But when she spoke, her words were simple and tinged with pain.

"I was once a boy like you," she said, "and now I am an acolyte of the Order. Soon it will be your turn to stand and be Chosen, or not Chosen, as the Divine wills it. And no matter what the outcome of the choosing, you will all change, in one way or another. Some of you will not be happy with the decision. One or two of you might even try to take matters into your own hands." She looked each of the boys in the eye in turn. "I am here today to tell you, quite simply—don't. And if the prospect of being eaten alive by the white wolves does not deter you, then perhaps this might."

Liana stepped forward and crouched in front of what appeared to be a large bundle of rags at the foot of the tree and shook it gently. The bundle unfolded to reveal something that might once have been human. Its flesh hung in great greasy folds like melted candle wax. Clumps of hair sprouted in random patches on its malformed limbs. It caught sight of the children and opened its toothless mouth wide, letting out a sound somewhere between a gurgle and a roar and lunging at them with outstretched hands, only to be brought up short by a chain encircling its ankle. Several children screamed in fright, the ones closest to the front pressed back against their classmates, and a few burst into tears. The wolves whined, and one of them rose to pad forward and nudge the creature back from the children. It licked at a smudge of dirt on the thing's face as if it were a wolf cub.

Callum shook his head. Sten had been tall and strong and smart and handsome. This...thing could not possibly be Sten.

"It wasn't always this way. The Order's archives show that there was once a time when we didn't even need the pesago tree, when women were born, not made."

Callum's mouth fell open in shock. That could not be true either. Surely this whole day was some cruel practical joke. The priestess allowed herself a little smile, lending weight to Callum's suspicions.

"Hard to imagine, I know," she said. "Then things changed. Nobody knows how or why. Lucky we discovered the pesago tree, or none of us would be alive today.

"There was also once a time when bringing on the Change was as simple as plucking the fruit from the tree and eating it. That too changed over time. The Order exists to keep the knowledge of the exact nature and proportions of the ingredients of the pesago potion. Too much of this, too little of that, drink the wrong amount or at the wrong time, and your transformation will go wrong. Eat the pesago fruit straight from the tree and this is what will happen to you." She indicated the creature that was now gnawing at a tree root and drooling happily.

"That is all. You may leave now." The boys scuttled back to the sanctuary of the temple as quickly as they dared.

They were uncharacteristically subdued as they made their way back to their classroom, none more so than Callum. His classmates were well aware of his relationship to the creature under the pesago tree, and they seemed to avoid him as a consequence. Callum pressed his mouth into a hard line and said nothing.

He didn't care what that bitch priestess said, or what the Order tried to make him do. He was never going to change.

Never, ever, ever.

The Oldest Profession

I feel it as soon as he enters the room. It's more intense than ever before, and although the client is nervous, I'm shaking worse than he is, shaking like a strung-out junkie. He takes out his wallet and says something to me, but the buzzing in my head is so loud that I can't make out exactly what he is saying. He fans out several twenty-dollar bills in front of me, a quizzical look on his face.

"Later," I say. I'm breaking Rule Number One. "We'll talk about payment later."

I never come when I'm with a client, but his bare skin sliding on mine magnifies the feeling of prescience until I reach a climax of a kind, a glorious mind/soul fuck that stops just this side of agony. I stifle a scream, digging teeth and nails into his shoulders. Seconds later he finishes, rolls off me and looks at his watch.

"Oh, shit," he says, "I've gotta go. How much do I owe you?"

"The placenta of your first-born child," I say. "The baby girl that will be born in six days and seventeen hours."

He stares at me, his hand frozen in mid-air over his wallet on the side table. I am suddenly very, very tired. Tired of fucking strangers for money, tired of trying to explain myself to guys like this, tired of this intermittent foresight that only brings me grief.

But it's no use fantasizing about a nice safe office job. I was literally born for this life, courtesy of my mother's bloodlines. For countless generations, the women in my family have worn the tainted labels of our calling. Witch. Sorceress. Prophet. Bitch goddess. Harlot. Whore.

"Look," I say. "I'm only trying to help. Your baby has a serious illness. The doctors won't be able to do anything, but if you bring me that placenta, I can cure her."

He has one leg in his trousers and hops frantically around the room looking for his shoes.

"If that baby dies, your wife Gail will never get over it. And neither will you, Michael." His hand is on the door handle. I mention their names only to convince him that I am legit, but it comes out sounding like a threat.

"What will you do if I don't do what you want?" he says.

"Nothing," I say. So very, very tired... "But you will do it. When you see how sick your baby is, you'll do it."

Thankfully, my week has been free of flash-forwards, but come Friday night, I get that familiar tingling on the back of my neck. That's just great, my client hasn't even made it into the room yet, and I'm feeling it already. The tingling starts to prickle, and then it turns into a burning sensation. I was wrong. This is not the beginning of a prescient episode. This is something far worse.

He comes in without knocking. His features are indistinct, and it's not just the tears of pain in my eyes that are blurring my vision; he shimmers with a dark glamour. He is tall and powerfully built, and he moves with preternatural speed as he crosses the room and pins me face down on the bed. His tongue flickers against my earlobe, leaving a searing pain in its wake. I smell charred flesh, and I squirm uselessly under his weight.

"I've been lonely without you, Wendy. Please...take me back."

It's no surprise he was able to stroll through all my protective spells as if they were walls of tissue paper, because, in a sense, he is me. He's the ugliest parts of my psyche made manifest. I cast this demon out of myself years ago, yet here he is, bigger and stronger than ever. I wonder what, or who, he's been feeding on during our time apart.

He trails sharp fingernails up the back of my thigh, rips my panties aside, and tries to regain admittance in the crudest way possible. Despite the pain, I almost laugh. Rape? Like that's going to work. He forces his way into every orifice, as if he has suddenly grown two extra pairs of appendages, poking and scratching and tearing. He plugs my nostrils shut, and forces something large and pulsating down my throat. I gag and flail against the bed, wasting the last gasps of air in my burning lungs.

Then he is gone. I drag myself to the head of the bed, push the panic button on the wall, and sit, breathing deeply and dripping blood. It takes approximately twenty-five seconds for the bouncers to burst through the door. I wince when I see the slideshow of emotions play across their faces at the sight of me— horror, revulsion, anger, and a trace of pity. This is going to hurt like fuck in the morning.

I'm not surprised to hear that they didn't pass anyone in the hallway. One of them calls for an ambulance, while the other heads off to check the security cameras, but I already know they will show nothing but haze.

Michael arrives outside the brothel just after 11 pm the next night. He clutches a small cooler bin to his chest. I step out of the alleyway and grab his arm.

"Over here," I whisper. My throat is still raw from the night before. Michael jumps and starts to pull away, until he sees my face.

"Jesus!" he says. "What happened to you?"

"Jesus had nothing to do with it," I say. "What did you call her?"

"Huh?"

"Your daughter. What did you call her?"

Even although he has obviously had a shit of a day, with no sign of improvement, he smiles. "Sophie."

"Sophie," I repeat to myself. I get a flash of foresight, an image of a smiling, dark-haired girl sitting on a swing, her little sandaled feet brushing the earth on each downward arc. You must be Sophie. She turns her head as if she hears me calling to her through the years.

"She looks like you," I say as I take the bin from his arms and limp away.

I don't know on a conscious level how this shit works. Like the visions, the knowledge comes to me when it wants to. I just stand back and let my body do what it is told. For years I've been saving a little something from every client I've ever serviced, without knowing why. Usually it's semen, but I've also got strands of hair, and even dried blood. No fancy cauldrons for me—I gather up all the samples and put them into an electric frying pan. As they start to sizzle, I take the placenta from the cooler bin, slice it up into bite-sized pieces, and add them to the mix. Nonsense-sounding words are popping into my head, and the back of my neck begins to burn again, but I ignore it, concentrating on repeating and pronouncing the words correctly.

My front door gives way with a huge whomph, as if it's been hit with a percussion bomb. He's here, and he's not pissing around. I've recited enough of the spell to create a barrier around myself, and the placenta gives it enough potency to hold him at bay. He throws himself against the invisible wall and howls with rage, no longer bothering to conceal his true appearance. I look away, choke back the vomit rising in my throat, and stir faster.

"Wendy! Wendy!"

He's not howling now. He's begging, pleading for his life, and the voice he is using is familiar. Against my better judgment, I turn to look at him.

Oh, you bastard.

No wonder the voice is familiar. He's taken on the form of my brother Nigel. He holds his arms outstretched, palms upward. Blood drips onto the floor from deep gashes in each wrist. His eyes are wide with pain.

"Help me, Wendy!"

"Nigel's dead. Nice try, asshole." I stab my palm with a paring knife and hold it over the frying pan, adding another ingredient to the stew. He morphs into a monster, then back to my brother, then through a kaleidoscope of forms, all crying, all bleeding.

The spell is complete, or at least it should be. I see Sophie on her swing again. She's not smiling anymore; she looks sad and resigned. As I raise my fingertips to give her a little wave, she turns away, and the vision begins to fade.

I don't have enough power to make the spell work. Overcome with exhaustion, I slump to the floor and press my cheek against the cool floorboards. On the other side of the barrier, my personal demon mirrors me. We eye each other across the invisible divide.

Correction—I don't have enough power to make it work on my own. What I am about to do might be my last act of decency, so I may as well make it a good one.

I crawl through the dust, open up my arms, and welcome him back in.

Drive, She Said

Tony hasn't been a taxi driver for going on 14 years without developing a sixth sense about his fares. This one, he decides, is trouble with a capital T. Without a word, she slides into the front passenger seat bum first and swings two stiletto-clad feet inside after her. Her glossy leather skirt rucks up her thighs as it squeaks across the cheap vinyl upholstery. Her blouse is perilously low-cut. Between her breasts nestles a silver scimitar-shaped pendant. A tiny black tattoo adorns one slender ankle.

"No smoking in the cab," he says sharply, then blinks, confused. He could have sworn…but there is no cigarette, neither between her lips nor in her gloved hands. He shakes his head. *I'm getting too fucking long in the tooth to be working the graveyard shift.*

"Too many foreigners driving cabs in this city," she says. "Don't you think?" Her face is shrouded in shadow.

So she's going to be one of those *passengers…* Tony presses his lips together in a thin line.

"I got no problem with them," he says.

"What about you…"—she leans forward to examine his ID card—"Tony… Where are you from?"

"Born and bred here," he says, pointing at the ground. "Never been outside the city." It's a perverse point of pride for him. He senses the woman smile in the dark.

"Good, good," she says. "I need someone who took his first steps on this soil to give me safe conduct."

He's used to hearing all kinds of racist comments in his line of work, but this is the most oddly phrased. *Fruit loop*, he thinks.

"Tell me, Tony," she continues, "...have you been a taxi driver for long?"

"All my adult life," he says.

"And your father—what was his profession?"

He wants to say, *none of your fucking business*, but instead he finds himself answering her.

"My father? He was a cab driver too. A good man, my father was. Good provider."

"And his father before him?"

"What? Why...look, if you must know, he was the skipper of a passenger ferry."

The woman claps her hands delightedly. "Oh, the stars *are* in alignment tonight! I have found myself a true ferryman."

No, just the grandson of a ferryman, you mad bitch, Tony thinks. Annoyed now, he turns on the interior light and gets a good look at her face for the first time. She's hot, beautiful even, with full lips and sculptured nose and high cut cheekbones, her features reminiscent

(heatshimmersand)

of some unidentifiable distant shore. Not that that'll cut any ice with him. He gets propositioned at least twice a week, "a ride for a ride" they laughingly call it at the depot, but he's a good family man, got a wife and two kids at home, and besides, he's not that stupid.

He taps the sign on the dashboard.

"Fare has to be paid in advance, love," he says. "New rules and all that." He steels himself for dissent—she doesn't carry a handbag, nor can he see any pockets from which she can produce cash—but her hands flick through the air like a conjuror's, and two notes flutter into his lap. He picks them up and examines them.

Two hundred dollars.

"How far you wanting to go?" he asks. "'Cos I haven't got much change..."

"Just drive," she says. Her voice is low, silky, devoid of accent. She waves in the general direction of the meter. "Drive until the money runs out."

He hesitates, and she pouts mockingly at him.

"Come now, you are a true ferryman, are you not? A true ferryman would not turn away a passenger who bears the right coin." She winds down the window and sniffs the air like a

(cat)

dog. He opens his mouth to tell her not to, it's freezing outside, then she turns and looks at him

(eyes, black, so black)

and his protest dies unspoken.

"Take me somewhere dangerous," she says, and before he even realises, he's put the car in gear and is pulling away from the kerb.

Despite the icy air blasting through the open window, he is perspiring, feverish, and he dashes the sweat out of his eyes with the back of one hand. He wants to ask *what do you mean, somewhere dangerous?* But he knows, or at least his gut does, and he steers the cab toward the part of town where cops and taxis fear to tread.

This chick gives him the creeps, although he would be hard-pressed to say exactly why. He desperately wants her out of his cab, but with her two hundred dollars

(slave, in chains, with whip-striped back)

she has bought him, at least for the next couple of hours. Unless she does something illegal or destructive, he's stuck with her.

He drums his fingertips on the steering wheel.

"So…you just got off work, have ya?"

As soon as the words have left his mouth, he regrets them. At 3 a.m. and dressed like that, there's only one line of work she could be in. Whether she's a prostitute or not, she will resent the assumption. Normally he doesn't give a shit if he offends his customers with his 'banter', but this one…no, he really does not want to piss her off.

Mercifully, the implication goes over her head. That, or she doesn't care what he thinks of her.

"No," she says absently, "I'm…looking for something."

Aren't we all, love, aren't we all.

They travel in silence for several kilometres. The streets gradually become more dimly lit, more strewn with debris, and the buildings degenerate as they pass until it seems like the graffiti is the only thing holding them up.

"Down there," she commands, arm outstretched through the open window. "Slowly. Very slowly."

It goes against every instinct to kerb crawl in this part of town, but she is right; it would take more than a rough neighbourhood to make him turn down two hundred bucks. He glances anxiously about him. Over half the streetlights are broken. The denizens of the night, the drugged, deranged and down-on-their-luck, find shelter in doorways and side alleys. The street opens up abruptly into a plaza, its paving cracked and filthy, probably built as part of some urban beautification project that has spectacularly failed. It reminds Tony incongruously of a fairy circle in the woods, with bird shit-splattered concrete seats and sagging, half melted rubbish bins forming the outer ring.

"Stop," she says, holding up a palm. "Wait."

Stop? Here? Are you fucking nuts?

The sensible, if self-serving, thing to do would be to take off the instant she gets out of the cab. But he'd never abandon a fare, especially not a lone woman. He puts the car into neutral and hauls on the hand brake, but keeps the engine running. Anxiously, he caresses the baseball bat mounted on the inside of the driver's door.

The woman peels off her gloves and places them on the dash-board, then opens the door and steps out. The rhythmic click of her heels on the pavement draws out half a dozen deadbeats. Tony holds his breath.

Like prisoners emerging from a dungeon into daylight they come, cowering and blinking, hesitant hands reaching out to her. She passes her own hands palm downward over their heads as if in benediction. One barefoot man weeps. She whispers into one supplicant's ear, then another. They pass the message amongst themselves and disperse much more quickly than they came. The woman stands alone in the glow of a single functioning street light and waits.

A few minutes later, the roller door on a nearby derelict work-shop rattles open, making Tony jump and curse. A man emerges and approaches the woman. He is not like the others, not a patient failed by the mental health system, not an addict, or if he is, his addiction is not physical. He is

(magnificent)

straight-backed, clean, proud. Beneath a black leather vest he is shirtless, leanly muscled and seemingly impervious to the cold. His skin gleams as if oiled.

He and the woman could be brother and sister.

The man stops a few paces from the woman and opens his arms wide in a gesture that is part welcome, part challenge.

"You did not have to send them to fetch me," he says. At this distance, Tony should not be able to hear him clearly, yet his voice is as distinct as if he sat in the passenger seat. The man says the woman's name, or at least, that's what Tony assumes he says, because in that instant the acoustics of the place go screwy, and it's like he is listening to a not-quite-correctly-tuned radio station broadcasting in a foreign language.

"I felt you here. I would have come anyway. What—did you think I would be afraid?" The man arches one eyebrow and crosses his arms across his chest. He flicks a glance in Tony's direction.

"You! Ferryman!"

Wish all these nutcases would stop calling me 'ferryman,' Tony thinks.

"How much did she pay you? Whatever it was, it was not enough."

Tony smirks. *What is this, a B grade movie?* He half-expects the man to offer him double. *Take me back to the city,* he imagines him saying. *Leave that bitch behind.*

The woman murmurs something, lowers her gaze and shakes her head. A message has passed between the pair, the import of which eludes Tony. For a moment he thinks she is defeated.

And then she laughs.

The man backs away, looking far more terrified than he should at the sound. Tony sympathises; he feels it too, a primal fear chilling his bowels, as if he has suddenly come face to face with a snarling tiger. The woman moves with preternatural speed to close the gap between her and the man. Gentle as a lover, she places her hands on either side of his head and leans in to kiss him on the lips. Again Tony gets the impression of smoke, swirling from the corners of the woman's mouth and obscuring his vision.

Although the man's mouth is still covered by hers, he screams. It is like

(nailsonblackboardrabbitinatrap)

nothing Tony has ever heard before. Years later, Tony will almost convince himself that it was a hallucination, a mere trick of the light exacerbated by fatigue. But right here, right now, he sees the man turn inside out. Skin splits. Bones splinter. Muscles contract wetly. Brain and heart and lungs and intestines hover untethered in mid-air.

Then the illusion is over. The man is whole and unmarked. The woman releases him and steps back. For a couple of heartbeats, his eyes stare blankly over her shoulder. His mouth lolls open. Then he collapses to the ground, his crumpled form somehow diminished by more than just his state of unconsciousness.

The woman strolls back towards the cab. She licks her lips, her tongue quick and furtive.

Then she begins to lick her fingertips clean.

By the time she resumes her seat, Tony is gibbering.

"Is he dead? He's...you...I saw...the scream...he must be... should we call someone? He's dead, isn't he? Isn't he?"

The woman shrugs. She examines her fingernails and touches the tip of her tongue to one tiny remaining speck of red. Apparently satisfied, she slides her hands back into her gloves.

"Yes. No. Depends what you mean by 'dead'." She swivels in her seat toward him, her knees pressed primly together and all-but-touching his trembling hand on the gear stick.

"You have been a good servant, Tony. Faithful. Honest. Obedient. I like that. And you have served me in two capacities, both as my driver and by bearing witness of my judgment. You shall have your reward." She leans forward and presses her lips to his cheek. The gesture is strangely ritualistic.

The kiss of death... Tony is instantly awash. He sobs and trembles like a nightmare-stricken child. Snot bubbles from both nostrils. He loses control of his bladder, and the acrid aroma of urine fills the cab.

"Oh, look," the woman says, pointing at the meter, "time's up."

It can't be, the still rational part of his mind insists, *we haven't been out nearly long enough,* but when he looks, it is just in time to see the meter click over. Two hundred dollars exactly.

She smiles. Kisses her fingertips and waggles them at Tony. Steps out of the cab and melts away into the dark.

After That Fare, as he thinks of it, things are different for Tony. Belligerent customers suddenly turn meek and deferential within the confines of the cab. Nobody tries to mug him or to do a runner. One young tough, on discovering his wallet empty at the end of the ride, bursts into tears and offers him his watch, his cell phone, the virginity of his sister, anything, only please don't, please don't...

Don't what? Turn you inside out?

The fear in the young man's eyes sickens Tony, and he waves him away, sending him stumbling for the safety of home.

His dreams are haunted by the memory of what he saw, or thought he saw. Sometimes he is merely the observer, sometimes the victim, sometimes the perpetrator. The only way to stop it, he reasons, is to return to the scene. But it is several months before he finds the courage to do so, and even then, he can only face it in the middle of the day. In the light it is a different place, mundane and harmless. It is deserted save for two council workers in fluoro vests who lean against their truck and share a cigarette. Tony is faintly surprised not to find the man still lying where he fell.

The feeling of her kiss on his cheek never completely departs. It's a slight, localised sensation, like someone is perpetually blowing on his face through a straw. Some days he even thinks he can see the outline of her lips on his skin.

That's the reason, he thinks, tapping his reflection in the mirror. He scrubs uselessly at the mark until his face is rubbed raw.

Faithful. Honest. Obedient. That's my reward.

Father Figure

I met her during rush hour on a wintry Friday afternoon on the steps of Flinders Street Station. She stood slightly apart from her friends, an outcast amongst outcasts. Commuters migrating homeward bumped and jostled each other in the crush, yet the crowd instinctively parted to leave the little coven of goths inviolate.

Untouchables. That's what they appeared to be. That's what I once was, before I grew up, got responsible, jumped on the corporate gravy train. Yet one look at Mia and all I wanted to do was touch her. Touch her in the most intimate and urgent ways, shake her, bruise her, drive her to her knees, wipe that sullen look off her face and replace it with one of flush-faced, open-mouthed, uncontrollable lust, run my hands through her long, black hair and pull real tight…

The impulse shook me; I considered myself a lover, not a fighter, and certainly not both at once. And right then I should have heeded my inner caution and walked on. But instead I stared at her, willing her to meet my gaze, and she did for a split second before turning away with a sneer. As well she should, for I was nearly twice her age and should have no business looking at her with the thoughts I was having. I was no stranger to sexual conquest, albeit with women closer to my own age and social milieu, but there was something…*different* about this girl. I dithered on the steps, pretending to fish around in my pockets for something and trying like a lovelorn teenager to pluck up the courage for a direct approach. Surreptitiously, I studied her more closely.

She wore the traditional goth costume; head to toe in black. Despite the cold, her shirt was sleeveless, made of a flimsy lace material that allowed tantalising glimpses of pale skin. I smiled — no doubt she rebelled against everything, even the weather. She turned to talk to a friend, thus affording a clearer view of the black-inked pseudo-Celtic tattoo adorning one bicep, and my smile widened — there was my opportunity. As I closed the gap between us, I bolstered my confidence with a mental image that I couldn't fully buy into; I was the Big Bad Wolf, and she my Little Black Riding Hood.

"I'm Andy," I said, extending a hand. She looked at it as if I had just offered her a plate full of dog shit. Only slightly deterred, I pushed on. "That's an interesting tattoo. Do you know what it means?"

"Of course I do," she spat, "but I'm not going to tell you."

"You don't need to," I said. "I know what it means. It means that we're destined to be together." A battle waged in my head: *Could you get any more cheesy?* versus *But what if it's true?* The latter won out, and I leaned closer and lowered my voice.

"I have an identical tattoo."

"Bullshit," she said. Her gaze flickered from my face to my suit-clad arms and back again. For an instant her aloof exterior cracked, and I saw something akin to hope in her eyes. Hope that I might be The One, that I might succeed where others had failed (or perhaps not even attempted) to save her from whatever misery her life contained. No longer the Big Bad Wolf, I became the Knight in Shining Armour. Now *that* was a role I could sincerely play.

"C'mon," I said. "It's cold out here. Let's go somewhere to warm up and I can show you." This time, she accepted my outstretched hand.

And so, over a couple of glasses of absinthe in a dimly lit corner of an impossible-to-find-unless-you're-in-the-know back alley bar, I shrugged off my jacket and tie and slid my business shirt down over my shoulder to reveal her tattoo's twin. It wasn't really any great coincidence — no doubt she'd chosen the design the same way I had twenty years ago, by pointing at a picture on a tattoo parlour wall—but she was suitably impressed all the same. From the moment her fingertips caressed my inked skin, she was mine.

While a part of me still screamed *Wrong! Wrong! Wrong!* I slid quickly into love, in spite of—or perhaps, because of—her troubled background. Mia's drug-addicted mother had died from an overdose when she was a toddler, and nobody knew who her father was. She'd been raised by a series of indifferent foster parents—so beautifully damaged, a wild, rudderless child. When she told me seven months later that she was pregnant, I was jubilant, and proposed to her on the spot. Everybody counselled us against getting married. Everyone, that is, who cared, which was precious few.

Was I drawn to her youth? Yes. Her fragility? Yes. Did I want to protect her, to save her, from herself and the world at large? Yes. Was I tired, bored and lonely, and looking to stave off the oncoming ravages of old age a little longer with a vital young wife? Yes. Did we rush into our marriage, with little thought for the consequences? Yes. Yes, yes, a thousand times yes, yet all these tawdry truths did not come close to describing the profundity of our relationship. We were *connected* on some deep, indefinable level that transcended the clichés of our union.

The change in Mia became evident almost immediately after we got engaged. She put away the trappings of her misery—the thick black eyeliner, her exclusively black clothing, her extensive collection of drear, moody so-called music. The scars on her limbs from her self-harming episodes faded. Her eyes sparkled. She *smiled.* I was vindicated in my love and support. She carried and gave birth to our child with a joy and ease that other women envied. Bain, we named him, and he was perfection incarnate. Certain that nothing could spoil our happiness, we scheduled our wedding to coincide with Bain's first birthday.

On the eve of our wedding she came to me bearing a battered shoe box.

"Burn it," she commanded, a glimpse of her former, defiant self flashing across her face as she thrust it into my hands.

"What is it?" I asked.

She shrugged. "Photos. Letters. Documents. Mostly old shit that belonged to my mother. None of it means anything to me anymore. You and Bain are my only family now." She rested one hand on her belly, not yet swollen with our newly conceived second child.

I cradled the box in my lap as if it might contain a venomous snake. "Well, if you're sure..."

"I'm sure."

She did not say 'don't open it', and even if she had, I would have disregarded her. When she left for the night to attend to whatever mysterious wedding rituals women observe, I removed the lid and examined the first item. It was Mia's birth certificate; despite her instructions, I set it aside against some future need. There were a few blurry, poorly composed photos of a teenaged girl who I assumed was Mia's mother Debbie. I studied them closely. The quality of the photos made it hard to learn anything from them; she looked familiar, and I was caught in an uncomfortable state of not-quite-recognition, unable to tell whether I knew her from a former time or was merely acknowledging the features she shared with her daughter.

I turned to the other items. Old concert ticket stubs, a lock of jet-black hair barely held together with ancient, yellowing sticky tape, a cheap necklace bearing a small, blue stone pendant which I threw into the bin...they meant no more to me than they did to Mia.

At the bottom of the box sat a bundle of letters bound with a rubber band. I skimmed through the first few. They were almost laughable in their banality—badly written old love letters penned by adolescent admirers, and one angry missive from Debbie's mother over some long forgotten grievance—and I was almost ready to toss the entire bundle back into the box, when something about the last letter caught my attention. It was from a young man, begging Debbie to abort, adopt out, pin the blame on someone else, say she was raped, do *anything* other than name him as the father of her unborn child. His life would be ruined otherwise, he claimed with staggering selfishness.

I knew the handwriting only too well, although I'd long since forgotten the circumstances that had prompted the letter, buried as they were beneath so many other careless close calls of my youth. I sat and stared at the pages for what seemed like hours. Big Bad Wolf indeed; I felt like I had been hollowed out and my stomach filled with stones that weighed me down until I could no longer move.

Then came the self-justifications. Perhaps it was a mistake. Perhaps this was just some horrible coincidence, this Debbie not the same one that I had once known, but some other callous youth's discard. Or perhaps it was my Debbie, but not my child. After all, she could have slept with any number of young men that summer, as free with her affections as I conveniently remembered her to be. Yes, that must be it; after all, wasn't Bain's robust good health and beauty living proof that Mia could not be my daughter?

I looked at the birth certificate again, at the "Father: Unknown." With one word, Debbie had both saved and condemned me. Still, a DNA test would settle the question, and it wasn't too late to postpone the wedding. And yet…

My favourite game as a child had been to 'hide' by covering my eyes with my hands; if I could not see my hunter, I reasoned, then he or she could not see me. It had always served me well as a problem-solving strategy and I saw no need to give it up now. I burned the box with its damning letter inside, and kept my mouth firmly shut about it. I was probably the only person alive who so much as suspected the truth of Mia's parentage, and I buried that suspicion deep down until it became as ephemeral a thought in my consciousness as the smoke that rose from the embers in the fireplace.

After Bain came Layla, then Charlize, Sebastian, and finally Poppy. Five beautiful, healthy children under the age of seven and all of them with the same black hair, pale skin and delicate features. Like a household full of Snow Whites, our neighbours used to say. After Poppy, I booked myself in for a vasectomy, citing a long list of sensible reasons, but in truth I did it because I feared that we were pushing our luck. Every pregnancy brought with it a deep anxiety on my part that the child would be born malformed in some way; it felt like we were playing Gestational Russian Roulette. Mia was happy enough with my decision, as you would expect for the mother of five. Our lives were cheerfully chaotic, and we immersed ourselves in love and a deep contentment. My family kept me feeling young, but they could not stop the physical signs of aging, not that I cared much about that anymore. I grew round of belly and grey of hair, and the only time it bothered me was when strangers mistook me for the children's grandfather. Too close to the bone by far, these innocent assumptions made me want to prove my vitality by throttling the life out of them.

The cracks began to appear when Bain turned fourteen. Literally overnight, he changed from a happy, if slightly highly strung, child to a surly and uncommunicative teenager. I was unconcerned; my own adolescence had been much the same, and I had come out the other side of it relatively unscathed (*not so for Debbie*, my subconscious whispered, and I squashed down the thought).

But for Mia, the change in her first-born child sparked off her own, cataclysmic shift in outlook.

"There must be something wrong with him," she said, chewing on a thumbnail. She hadn't chewed her nails in fifteen years, and I resisted the urge to slap her hand away from her face. "Some hormonal imbalance or something."

I laughed. "Of course it's a hormonal imbalance! It's called puberty. He'll settle down eventually…just give him time."

"But still, it's not normal…is it?"

She ignored my reassurances, and became convinced that, not only Bain, but our entire family was in the grip of some mysterious malady. Mia marched us all, one by one, to the family doctor, and when she pronounced us all in robust good health, Mia sought a second opinion. And a third. She took our temperatures twice a day, and seemed almost disappointed at the invariably normal results. Every blemish, every cough, every little twinge became the subject of intense scrutiny. She visited dermatologists, chiropractors, dieticians and acupuncturists, dragging with her whichever child she could coerce at the time. A visit to the naturopath had her imposing on the family an organic diet free of meat, soy, dairy, gluten, wheat and sugar. A task as simple as mopping the floor set off a paroxysm of indecision, as she was unable to choose between scouring away potentially deadly bacteria and exposing her family to toxic chemicals.

The children had always been closer to their mother than to me, but Mia's obsession skewed the family dynamic in a different direction. I became their ally, their confidant and their accomplice as I snuck them out of the house on various pretexts to gorge ourselves on burgers and fries, slipped them extra cash to stock their school lunch boxes with more desirable items, invented alibis to get them out of medical appointments, or simply provided them with adult conversation that did not revolve around their health.

One day I caught Bain smoking behind the garden shed. A normal response would have been to punish the child, deliver a stern lecture and confiscate the cigarettes. But we were in no normal situation. Instead, I merely sighed and helped myself to a cigarette out of the packet. I leaned against the shed wall and lit up, inhaling smoke into lungs that had not been abused in such a fashion for the better part of fifteen years.

I smiled at Bain. "Don't tell Mum," I said.

"I won't," he said, smiling back. We finished our smokes in silence and luxuriated in our guilty camaraderie.

"I went to see a psychic today," Mia said one evening. It was the end of a particularly trying week; the children had gone from sly avoidance to open defiance whenever their mother tried to drag them off to some specialist or another, and Mia was angry at me for taking their side.

"And?" I pretended mild indifference, keeping my eyes on the TV screen as I channel surfed without taking any of it in. There was something in her tone that made my hackles rise, and I steeled myself for another confrontation.

"The spirits told her that my intuition has been right all along, and that we have some hereditary disease. Something genetic. It's rare, she says, and the symptoms haven't manifested yet, which is why it hasn't been diagnosed. Apparently, we're all ticking time bombs. She says I should go back to the doctors and request DNA testing."

DNA testing...panic made me explode. I leapt up from my seat, grabbing her by the shoulders and dragging her to her feet, and shook her until her teeth rattled.

"For fuck's sake, Mia, this has got to stop! We're all fine! We don't need DNA testing, or any other kind of testing! The only one sick around here is you—sick in the head."

I regretted my words the instant I uttered them. It was what we had all been thinking, or muttering behind Mia's back, but been afraid to voice for fear of making her worse. I expected her to react with tears or anger, or both, but instead a curious calm came over her. She took a deep breath and shook her head, even giggling a little as she spoke.

"'A psychic told me...' Yeah, I can see how you might think that sounds a little crazy. Maybe I'm just stressed, or overtired. I probably just need a little break. A couple of days away on my own to get a bit of perspective."

"Yeah, maybe..." I drew her into a hug and muttered an apology into her hair. "I'll book you into a hotel somewhere nice," I promised. "Somewhere in the country, with a day spa." She nodded her assent, but the rigidity of her body told me that this was only a temporary truce, and the battle was far from over.

For a few months after Mia's getaway, things in our household were almost normal. She let up on the dietary restrictions, and there were no more unnecessary visits to medical practitioners. The children began to relax a little, although they still held their mother at a slight distance, as if she were a not-quite-tamed animal that could turn on them at any moment.

Then one night I came home from work to a cold, dark and silent house. I thought at first that everyone had gone out, so I jumped, startled, when I switched on a light to find Mia sitting at the kitchen table.

"What's going on? Where are the kids?"

"I sent them all to their rooms," she said. Her voice was strained, as if her throat were in the grip of a giant, unseen hand. She stared down at an opened envelope and several sheets of folded A4 paper on the table in front of her, turning the pages over and over reflexively, her face obscured behind a curtain of glossy, black hair. She lifted her head to look at me, her expression held unnaturally still.

"I had DNA testing done on all of us," she said. "I had to be sure."

I gripped the back of a chair to stop myself from falling. "How...how did you manage to do that without us knowing?"

She waved a hand in dismissal. "Oh, you'd be surprised where you can get DNA samples if you're trying to be secretive– toothbrushes, nail clippings, snot on a used tissue...saliva from cigarette butts..." she said, pointedly emphasising the latter. I had visions of her gathering her materials, not to conduct scientific tests, but to create voodoo dolls of us all.

She rose from her chair, suddenly incandescent.

"You knew, didn't you?" she yelled, punctuating each word by poking me in the chest with a sharp-nailed forefinger and sending me backpedalling into the kitchen bench. "I gave you that box of my mother's letters, and you must have read them, and you MUST have recognised yourself in that one letter, and you said NOTHING! You let me conceive all those babies, and you...you..." She stopped, speechless with rage and revulsion.

"I didn't know for sure," I protested. "I only suspected..." I glanced behind me, checking for any readily accessible weapons, not for myself but to keep them away from her; if she could reach a knife at that moment, she would surely plunge it into my heart.

The children, drawn out by the noise, emerged one by one from their various retreats about the house. They were all graceful and gorgeous, magnificent young creatures as they walked past their mother and came to stand at my side.

"'Suspected'? Just your suspicion alone should have been enough to end it. You should never have married me. I should have aborted Layla, drowned Bain in the bath and got as far the fuck away from you as possible." Spittle flew from her mouth and hit me in the face, but I did not wipe it away, my hands being too occupied trying futilely to shield my children's ears from her obscene rant.

At my shoulder, Bain stiffened. "What are you on about now, Mum?" he said scathingly. Mia looked at him as if seeing him for the first time. There was no rage left in her now, only a bone-deep despair.

"It's OK," I murmured to Bain. "I'll handle this." Poppy pressed closer to me and chewed on her thumbnail, just like her mother did in times of stress. Just like I had done at the same age.

"Look at them," I said to Mia, gesturing at our children. Except that with each passing moment they were becoming less *our* children and more *my* children. "How can you call them a mistake?"

And she did look, for long moments, assessing the physical and psychic distance between us. "They're just kids…" she muttered to herself, but whether the 'just' meant that they had yet to reach maturity or that, being only children, they had little value, I wasn't sure.

"OK, Andy," she finally said. "You want them so much? They're yours. For now. But they will grow up and come to understand what you have done, and then you'll lose them. Remember this—as soon as they turn eighteen, I will reclaim them." This last sentence she spoke with vehemence and ritualistic slowness, as if uttering a curse or casting a spell.

Then she turned and walked out of the house. It was the last time any of us saw her alive.

Mia had left the house empty-handed except for her car keys. She made no attempt to access bank accounts or contact friends, no witnesses came forward to say they'd seen her anywhere, and no body matching her description was ever found. The only trace of her was the car, which police found abandoned in a semi-industrial area some fifteen kilometres from our home. She had simply vanished off the face of the Earth. I took to visiting the site where they'd found the car in the vain hopes that I would find some hitherto undiscovered evidence there, or that she would reappear as magically as she had disappeared. The urine-soaked and graffiti-splattered alleyway yielded no clues, yet it became something of a weekly pilgrimage for me to go there; it was the closest thing I had to a grave. Sometimes I imagined I could hear her voice whispering at me from the darkest recesses of the alley, but it was only the wind stirring the leaves and the echoes from my memories.

As for the kids, I was at once relieved and disturbed at the ease with which they flowed to fill the space left by their mother. There should at least been tears or misbehaviour, but instead they acted as if she never existed, as if they had sprung, godlike, directly from my loins. They never asked why she left, and I never volunteered the answer.

In fact, they thrived without her. Mia's absence seemed to have removed the shackles from their potential; all of them clever young things before she left, they grew tall and gifted, excelling at school and each possessing a particular prodigious talent. Bain was a sports star, Layla a mathematician, Charlize a musician, Sebastian a writer and Poppy an artist. The future for all of them was blindingly bright.

We'd all forgotten Mia's parting words when, three days after Bain's eighteenth birthday, a drunk driver steered her car into his, killing him instantly. If I'd had concerns about my children's lack of emotion when their mother left, I needn't have worried; the remaining four shed tears aplenty at their brother's graveside, and continued to grieve extravagantly in the months after his death.

We lost Layla to meningitis, which she contracted whilst on a camping trip with friends. I barely let the remaining three out of my sight after that, not that they wanted to stray far from home anyway in the wake of such tragedies. Charlize in particular became very withdrawn. She slept a lot, and during her waking hours she took to playing one mournful note over and over again on her cello. I put the changes down to depression and grief, but it turned out they were caused by the brain tumour that killed her the day after her eighteenth birthday.

I continued my visits to 'Mia's Alley', as I privately called it. Some days as I stared into the darkness, the darkness stared back, the shadows shifting and coalescing for moments into shapes almost human before dissolving back into meaninglessness. The day before Sebastian turned eighteen, I went to plead my case.

"Please stop, Mia," I whispered, feeling ridiculous but continuing regardless. "You have three now; leave me Sebastian and Poppy. Or one of them, at least. Surely you can see how much we've suffered already."

The wind moaned in response. *Bargain with your own children's lives, would you?* it seemed to mock. *Go home, old man. Go home to your grief.*

We celebrated Sebastian's birthday by closing the curtains and huddling inside, eating canned food and lighting candles for our fallen, which I would blow out within minutes for fear of one toppling and setting fire to the house. Poppy and I took turns standing guard over Sebastian while he slept, and he complained about how creepy it was to have someone staring at him all the damned time.

Nine days later, he was still alive. For the first time since Bain died, I began to feel, if not happy, at least hopeful that Mia's curse had been broken, or perhaps never existed in the first place. We drew back the curtains and opened the windows to let in some fresh air – which is when a bee flew in the window and landed on Sebastian's neck. He couldn't have seen what it was, only felt it brush against his skin. I leapt to stop him but I was too late; he slapped at it, and yelped when it stung him.

He went into anaphylactic shock, and died before the ambulance could arrive. I racked my brain for memories of childhood injuries, but could not recall him, or any of the other children for that matter, ever being stung. This time at least I could be there to see my child take his last tortured breath, to usher him out of my arms and into his mother's, wherever she might be and in whatever form she had taken.

Which left Poppy. My youngest child, my daughter who was so much like Mia in looks, mannerisms and personality that sometimes it hurt to be around her. Poor Poppy, who endured more tragedy in her short life than anyone ought to suffer. And just like her mother, she simply walked out the door one day and never looked back. Unlike her mother, they found her body, splattered at the base of a multi-storey parking building from which she'd jumped; evidently she'd decided that if she had to die young, it would be on her terms. Bystanders who'd witnessed her plummet put her time of death at eighteen years after her birth, to the minute.

I went back to Mia's Alley one more time, at midnight—The Witching Hour—on the night of a new moon. The lighting was sporadic already in the area, but I took out the two closest street lights with a few carefully aimed rocks. The darkness was near absolute.

I felt rather than saw her at first, a tiny disturbance in the air currents and a sudden, sharp drop in temperature.

"Silly man," a barely audible whisper tickled my ear, "you didn't have to come here to find me." Substance formed around the sound, and there Mia stood. Her hair, her eyes, her spectral clothing that swirled and slid across her body like an unholy mist, were so black, they were somehow visible against the now insipid night.

"Where else would I find you?" I managed to croak.

"Anywhere there is death. Anywhere there is grief." Behind her, our children—*her* children now, I reminded myself—took shape, although not as distinctly as Mia; some kind of barrier separated us, insubstantial looking yet impenetrable for one like me whose heart still beat. Their features were just as I remembered them, but their *expressions*…no human could bear such pain and knowledge and live. They now knew the truth of their parentage, I could see it in their eyes, and they condemned me for it. More than that, it looked like they'd been condemned to exhume the bones from every family's closets and make their beds on them.

Perhaps that's what death was—the sudden weight of the

universe's most sordid secrets.

My every instinct told me to run, to get far, far away from these ghouls masquerading as my family. But hadn't I yearned for this moment of reunion, however twisted it might be, for years?

I laughed. The sound echoed dementedly off the concrete buildings around us. "Anywhere there is death and grief? If that were the case, you would have been with me all along."

Her smile flooded me with yearning and terror, and literally made me buckle at the knees. "I have been," she said, "you just didn't know how to see."

"So will I always see you now?"

"No, Andy," she replied. "But you'll see me again, when it's your turn to join us." Her children receded into the darkness, leaving her alone to gaze down on me, I thought perhaps in pity. But when her final words came, they were steeped in triumph:

"And that will not be for a long, long time."

Riding the Storm

Maggie was the first to see the woman when she walked into the pub on that Tuesday night at the height of summer. The air conditioning was on the blink, and nobody had the energy to do more than move their drinks from table to face and back again. Still, a tremor of discontent rippled through the gathering. The locals were like dogs when it came to greeting strangers; some were nervously excited, some cautiously antagonistic, and one or two would get so overwhelmed that they peed on the floor. Maggie remembered her first introduction to Wengarro eighteen years ago, and felt a surge of sympathy for her.

She was an odd, unhealthy-looking creature. It was as if someone had drawn her in charcoal. Everything about her was cast in shades of grey, from her long, lank, not-quite-black hair to sallow skin to her shapeless clothing that did nothing to conceal anorexic thinness. Only her eyes had any colour. They were a luminous blue, and they bulged, bulbous and moist, like a frog's. Despite her slumped posture, she moved with a curious grace.

Barry Norman was first on his feet. He was a big man, nudging on two metres tall and weighing around 110 kilos, and he dwarfed the slightly built newcomer.

"Storm, isn't it?" he said, extending a meaty hand. Puzzled, Maggie flicked a glance at the open doorway and the cloudless sky beyond. *Can't be a storm. This is the worst drought in 35 years. We would have heard...* Then she realised that 'Storm' was the stranger's name. Jill Harris leaned into Maggie and whispered a rapid, breathless commentary in her ear.

"Used to live in a caravan by the river on the old Stevens place. Girls were home schooled, I think. Just the mum and four daughters, never saw a dad around. Quadruplets, they were. They all had weather names, lemme think… Storm, Tempest, Zephyr and…Mistral, yeah, that was it. No surname. Strange people, hippy types, they kept to themselves a lot. Nobody knows where they came from or where they went. They just turned up one night and disappeared again ten years later when the girls were in their mid-teens."

"Look how much you've grown, darlin'," Barry continued. "It's been, what, 20 years since you lived here? How's your mum and your sisters?" A couple of people snickered. Everyone knew that he took a keen interest in all things female, not because he was a rampant sex maniac (that position in the town was already filled), but because he spent his Sunday evenings cross-dressing in specially designed women's clothing purchased at great expense during his biannual trip to Melbourne.

Jim MacNamara let loose his nervous tic of a laugh. "Storm, heh, heh, we could use one around here, heh heh." Nobody saw fit to respond. Jim talked to himself constantly, even, it was said, in his sleep.

Storm ignored Barry, her head swivelling to fix her gaze on Jim.

"Yes," she said. "Yes, you could." She spoke with an unusual inflection, almost as if she were singing the words, and Maggie found herself leaning closer to hear her. There was not a hint of humour or irony in her tone. Jill surreptitiously circled her finger in the air next to her head, miming 'crazy' at Maggie. Based on what Jill and Barry had said, Storm must have been in her mid to late thirties, but she could have been anywhere from 16 to 60. There was something inconstant about her features, so she could look old and haggard at one moment, eerily beautiful the next. It almost hurt to look at her.

Storm turned back to Barry. He withdrew his hand, still hovering in the air waiting to be shaken, then extended it again, then withdrew it again, rubbing it anxiously against his jeans.

"Er…um…ah…would you like a drink?"

Storm smiled. Even her teeth looked grey. She inclined her

head in acceptance and sat in Barry's seat while he fumbled in his pockets for cash.

Something in Jill's summary bothered Maggie.

Nobody knew where they came from or where they went.

Nobody knew.

She shook her head in annoyance. There were no secrets in Wengarro, only complicity in keeping them against outsiders. They passed by osmosis from neighbour to neighbour, until you couldn't remember how you came to know, you just...*knew.* It was bad enough that Maggie had never heard of Storm and her family before now. For her to have lived in Wengarro for ten years and still have this veil of mystery over her—well, in Maggie's mind, it just wasn't fair.

Storm held court, a washed-out queen presiding over her meagre kingdom, as one by one her subjects approached. Any goodwill Maggie might have felt towards her soured and curdled in her stomach.

The rumour mill started grinding almost immediately.

"Karen Dodds saw her coming out of Jason Bartlett's house at 2 o'clock in the morning."

"Really? I heard she was carrying on with old Clancy Thomas—right under the nose of his wife! He must be eighty if he's a day."

"She's not fussy, that one. You know she slept with the Olsen brothers? Both at the same time, too. And they're not even out of their teens yet."

"Well, I heard she was a lesbian. Didn't you see her and Felicity Samuels in the corner at Johnno's birthday party? Had her tongue so far down Fee's throat you'd think she was gonna choke on it."

Young, old, male, female, nobody, it seemed, was immune to Storm's dubious charms. It was as if she had bewitched everyone. They ought to run her out of town, Maggie thought. But that wasn't about to happen. Wengarro couldn't afford such vicious luxuries. Every human living within its borders meant another prop for the town's fragile subsistence economy. During the town's 150-year existence, it had harboured murderers and thieves, rapists and paedophiles. It was hardly going to baulk at one funny-looking little nymphomaniac.

Maggie answered the knock on her door one Sunday evening to find Storm standing on her doorstep. She slipped past Maggie and into her living room.

"Excuse me! Did I say you could come in?"

"Of course you didn't," said Storm. "Nobody ever says what they want around here, do they? I don't think they even know half the time."

"I'll tell you what I *don't* want. I don't want you in my house, you little sl..."

"I saved you until last," Storm interrupted. She leaned against the back of Maggie's couch, tilted her head on one side like a quizzical dog, and smiled.

"What? Why...what?"

Storm pushed away from the couch, rested her hands on Maggie's shoulders and kissed Maggie on the cheek. Maggie stood immobilised by shock as Storm trailed feathery kisses across her face to land finally on her lips. An unexpected wave of desire washed over her and she recoiled, stumbling backward until she fetched up against the wall. They contemplated each other for several long moments, Maggie wild-eyed and breathing hard with panic, and Storm still bearing her idiot savant smile. Finally, Storm breached the space between them, languidly extended her left arm and brushed her index finger across the thin fabric of Maggie's T-shirt, teasing her nipple erect. Maggie's knees buckled.

"No, no, no, no..."

Storm inched toward her with agonising slowness, as if Maggie were a wild animal that might bolt at any moment, and kissed her again. Maggie tipped her head back, pulled Storm's lips to her throat, and howled, a wordless, inchoate sound of confusion and lust. She was only dimly aware that she was weeping.

When she woke the next morning, Storm was gone. Maggie stayed in bed past noon, unwilling to think of the night before and unable to not think about it. Yes, it had been two years since her husband Simon died,

(killed himself, the coroner said different, but you knew, everybody knew, you drove him to kill himself)

two years since she'd had sex with anybody, but that was no excuse for what she and Storm had done…

What *had* she and Storm done?

The lovemaking had unsettled her, coming as it did after a lifetime of unquestioned heterosexuality. But that wasn't the most disturbing thing about the encounter. In the darkness of Maggie's bedroom, Storm's body had felt oddly fluid and changeable; she could have been making love with anybody, male, female or some curious fusion of the two. Storm had been calm and deliberate, breathing evenly through a series of movements that were ritualistic in their precision. With each climax, Maggie had felt as if Storm were removing something from her, and now its absence left an aching wound. The sex had served both as anaesthetic and scalpel.

Finally, Maggie gave up trying to make sense of things. She got up, showered and dressed, and made a sandwich which she took outside to eat on the patio. Deprived of their morning meal, the chickens in their pen clucked and strutted restlessly. Maggie sighed and pushed aside the sandwich as she looked out over the farm. It was an awkward size, too big to be run by one person and too small to both support her and pay a farm hand. She'd been willing enough to come here for the few months her husband Simon had said it would take to help out his aging father. She'd had a romantic vision of an extended rural holiday, idyllic in spring with baby lambs and freshly laid eggs and clean country air.

(but it wasn't like that at all, it was all piss and shit and dust and heat and blood and sickness and death and decay)

Then her father-in-law had died. It took longer than expected to settle his estate. Simon used up his extended leave from his job, and by then Wengarro had him anchored, back where he belonged.

And eighteen years later, nothing had changed. The chooks still needed feeding, the veggie garden needed weeding, the sheep needed drenching, the fence along the northern border of the farm needed repairs…

Maggie laughed. She had never wanted children, had made it plain to Simon right from the start, although he always hoped to change her mind. And now here she was, shackled to the farm by its neediness, as if it were one great, big, insatiable, eternal child.

Fuck it. She'd sell the place. She'd give it away, if she had to. It wasn't like she hadn't thought about it before, but this time she was really going to do it. There was an entire world beyond Wengarro's borders to choose from. She'd pack up and move away

(to where?)

and get a job somewhere

(doing what?)

and get out of this rut.

She realised with a jolt that in the entire time she had lived in Wengarro, she had not seen anyone leave permanently.

(only way out is in a wooden box, and even then you don't leave, just go back to the earth, right where it wants you)

The enormity of the idea struck her, and she felt suddenly, gut-wrenchingly agoraphobic.

She went back to bed instead.

During the week after Storm's visit, Maggie couldn't help keeping an ear out on the grapevine for any more news of her exploits. But the town was strangely silent on the subject. She seemed to have disappeared just as suddenly and inexplicably as she had arrived.

It was just past dusk the following Sunday, and Maggie was washing the dinner dishes, when a figure appeared in her back yard under the waratah tree. Maggie started in fright and dropped a glass on the floor, where it shattered. Heedless of the shards, she crossed to the dining room and flicked on the patio light switch with trembling fingers. The intruder blinked stupidly and raised an arm to shield against the harsh spotlight; it was Storm.

Or her identical twin sister, because this woman could not

possibly be Storm. She stood with her feet wide apart, braced for the weight of her enormous pregnant belly. The woman gathered up the sides of her grey slip dress, pulled it over her head, and cast it aside. She was naked underneath. Her breasts were distended and laced with thick blue veins, and her belly undulated as the foetuses inside her jostled for position. She turned her back on Maggie and leaned with her hands on the trunk of the tree. Every muscle in her back tensed, and with a gush of blood, a tiny infant slipped from between her legs to thud wetly into the dust.

By the time Maggie got outside, four more little bodies lay in the dirt. Somewhere in the depths of her terrified mind, she registered the fact that there were no umbilical cords or placentas, just five infants, expelled whole and distinct.

And blood. So much blood. It burst from Storm's body in great black-red gouts, pooling around the babies until they floated in it. Nobody could lose so much blood and live—in fact, Maggie realised, nobody could possibly contain so much blood to start with. Yet Storm stood, without a trace of pain or distress on her face, waiting placidly until the flow ebbed and stopped. Like a toddler at the beach fleeing an oncoming wave, Maggie backpedalled just out of reach of the lake of gore, then fell to her knees and retched. She had assisted at many difficult births with her livestock, and inwardly she cursed herself for being so weak, but this was

(wrong)

different, and she could not bring herself to cross the bloody divide separating her from Storm and her cursed offspring.

Storm leaned over the babies and examined them. She picked one up by the wrist. It dangled, limp and lifeless, in her grip.

"A boy," she said. "They never survive." She stood and flung it away into the shadows. Maggie's stomach turned afresh, and she skittered further backwards on her hands and knees, anxious to put something, anything, between her and this madwoman. Storm knelt next to the four remaining babies, who squirmed, strangely silent, in the muck. She bent and whispered in their ears, one by one, and the infant girls seemed to listen with adult intent, straining upwards to take in her words.

In concert, the babies curled up on themselves, returning to the pose they would have held in the womb. The blood around them receded towards them, as if they were drawing it into their bodies, and they began to swell and grow at an impossible rate, unfolding like flowers, until minutes later they stood staring down at her, four newborn girls the size and form of six-year-olds. Maggie shoved a grimy fist in her mouth to stifle her scream, desperately clinging to her last vestiges of sanity. The ground beneath her trembled; not an earthquake, it was subtler than that, as if the girls were ticks on the earth's skin and it sought to shake them off.

Storm was gone. Her dress still lay where she had dropped it, and her bloody footprints trailed off into the dark. Ignoring the girls, Maggie pushed herself to her feet, ran back into the house and returned with a flashlight. Storm would surely need medical attention, and even if she didn't, there was no way Maggie was going to let her abandon her children. She followed the footprints as they became fainter and fainter until they disappeared entirely in the middle of the paddock. A sound in the distance caught her attention, and she shone the torch after it, but even as she did she knew she would not find Storm. Instead, she spotted several sets of car headlights, moving at speed down the dirt road towards her farm.

She returned to the children, who looked up at her solemnly. They all looked slightly different from each other, but all were naggingly familiar. They looked nothing like Storm.

But they all had Maggie's eyes.

She herded the girls inside and tucked them up in her bed, bloody skin and all. "Sleep," she told them in desperation, and incredibly, they did, their eyes closing and their breath slowing almost instantly. Car tyres crunched on gravel in her driveway outside, and she flinched, but the girls were oblivious. She scrubbed fear-moistened palms on her shirt and rushed to answer the hammering on her door.

It seemed like half the town stood on her doorstep. Jill Harris led the delegation, clutching a .22 in a white-knuckled grip. They looked like the stereotypical posse of superstitious villagers, out to capture the beast; all they were missing were the pitchforks and flaming torches. Maggie took a deep breath to quell the hysterical laughter welling up in her.

"You seen Storm?" said Jill.

"What's this about?" said Maggie.

"Someone's been snitching. Cops busted Jase for his dope plantation this morning. They've taken Jim in as well. Reckon he's been fiddling with his stepdaughter. And there are others. Wengarro'll be a ghost town by the time the cops are finished with us."

"And I'm leaving Sandy." This from Clancy Thomas, who leaned heavily on his cane.

Maggie raised an eyebrow. "You've been bitching about Sandy for as long as I've known you, Clancy. How could that have anything to do with Storm?"

"It must be her fault," said Barry from the back of the crowd. "We were all doing fine before she came along. Now she's just stirred things up and…changed things. Changed us. Besides, she's damn near the only one with nothing to lose."

"I've seen her," Maggie said. "Acting real funny, prowling around my back fence." It was technically the truth. "I reckon you're right. She's been up to no good from the minute she came here." Several in the gathering nodded assent. "I went out to talk to her, but she took off over the paddock. She's probably halfway to the road by now. If you hurry you'll be able to head her off."

"Thanks, Maggie. You're a good sort." The crowd dispersed and headed off in search of the phantom Storm. Maggie stood guard, waving false good wishes until the last taillight winked out of sight around the bend. Only then did she dare to slump to the floor with despair.

Maggie didn't mind caring for Storm's children. They were as independent and aloof as cats, helping themselves to food from the pantry and wandering off for hours or days at a time. They always returned bearing gifts. It might be something pretty and impractical, like a bunch of wildflowers tied with a thick red ribbon, or a dusty, delicate silver bracelet. Or it might be something improbable but sorely needed; one afternoon at dusk she watched all four of them stagger up the driveway in single file with a five-litre petrol-filled jerry can in each hand. Another time one of them wordlessly handed her a large, grimy teddy bear that rustled strangely when she took hold of it. She slid down the zipper in its back to find it stuffed with bundles of fifty-dollar bills. Maggie never knew where their bounty came from, and she never asked.

Not that she would have received a straight answer. The girls seldom chose to speak. When they did, the meaning behind their utterances was elusive. After their extraordinary birth, they settled down into a conventional rate of growth. But Maggie could never quite trust that things would always be this way, so she kept a supply of clothes in a variety of sizes, just in case. She liked to read aloud to them from whatever book she was engrossed in at the time, and they liked to listen, sitting wide-eyed and serious on the end of her bed. Every now and again she considered giving them names, but the idea would no sooner occur to her then it would slip away again.

She liked her new home in Ilisford. It was much like Wengarro, which was probably why the girls had chosen it. She made no special effort to conceal the girls' existence from the town's inhabitants; whenever she made one of her infrequent visits into the township, someone would invariably enquire about the wellbeing of her 'daughters'. She would mumble an evasive answer, the enquirer's eyes would glaze over, and soon the topic would change to something safer. She recognised in their faces the same fuzzy-headedness that overtook her whenever she tried to focus her mind's eye on the girls.

That fuzzy-headedness came over her more and more often these days. The void that Storm had created in her was spreading like a cancer. It was hollowing her out, making her feel lighter, less earthbound, as if she could float away at any moment. She imagined her friends from Wengarro similarly afflicted, a flock of them untethered from the earth and drifting across the Queensland sky.

(except none of them had been your friends, not really)

It would happen again, she was sure of it; the girls would go out into the world, and one day, just like their birth mother had, one of them would return to Ilisford; perhaps to successfully tear the town apart, perhaps not. It was an endless battle between two ancient forces, the natures of which Maggie could never fully comprehend.

From time to time she felt Wengarro tugging at her, trying to drag her back. But as the girls grew older, the pull grew weaker. And even if she wanted to return, she could no longer remember the way.

Slither and Squeeze

"Snake! Snake!"

The old man's reedy voice cuts through the crowded train. He pulls himself into a ball, draws his feet up onto the seat and wraps his arms over his head. A couple of women scream and follow his example, lifting their feet off the floor and pulling their knees into their chests. A tremor of panic ripples through the commuters, and those closest to us press as far away as they can. The other passengers follow his terrified gaze to look at me. I study my reflection in the window, feigning indifference, but the weight of their attention is stifling.

My sister Lara slips out of her seat and kneels in front of the old man. She turns to our fellow travellers, raises her hand and lowers it palm down as if physically dampening down the tension. "Calm down, everyone, there's no snake," she says. "I'll handle this—I'm a mental health professional." She has no way of substantiating this, but they all seem to believe her. It's far easier for them to leave the old man in Lara's hands than to listen to his lunatic screech, or worse, to do something about it themselves.

Lara looks the old man in the eyes and speaks to him in a low, steady monotone. I can't hear what she is saying, but whatever it is, it seems to be working. His yells subside into a meaningless mutter before stopping altogether. Lara strokes his shin, tentatively at first but with increasing confidence as he responds to her touch and gradually unwinds himself.

I don't know what irritates me more—Lara the timid little mouse, which she is most of the time, or the confident in-charge

Lara, an act she pulls out every now and again, usually when I am not in a position to take back control.

Lara returns to her seat beside me. There is a smattering of applause on the train, which she acknowledges with a smile and a nod as if she were royalty.

I lean in and whisper into her ear.

"Nicely done. Looks like you've learned a trick or two from me on how to mesmerise people. Since you seem so intent on taking over from me, you have to kill him now."

Lara's smile does not falter. "Get fucked, Maxine," she whispers back.

"I'm serious, Lara."

"He's a crazy bag-man—nobody's going to believe him."

"We've been through this before. Imagine what could happen if he gets together a posse of his loony mates and comes after us. I'd do it myself, but..." I slide my sleeve up a couple of inches and show her the thick strip of skin sloughing off my arm, the fresh skin beneath pink and vulnerable.

"We don't need the attention? Speak for yourself, ya freak." She is no longer smiling. The train slows, then stops, the hiss of the opening doors startling the more herpetophobic passengers. Crazy bag-man gets off. Lara sighs and rocks in her seat for a few moments. "I'm just going to make sure he's OK," she says. She propels herself after him.

Fear is the universal emotion. We're all afraid right now—me, the old man, even my sociopathic sister, Maxine. It's my job to make sure that the fear doesn't make one of us do something stupid.

I was being straight up when I told her I was just looking out for the old guy. I know what it's like seeing things that aren't supposed to exist, although I don't have the dubious luxury of being able to explain it away as the product of mental illness. I step it up, drawing level with him and taking him by the elbow. He squeals like a girl and flaps out of my grip.

"Don't touch me! I saw you talking about me. You two are in cahoots." His face crumples in accusation.

"Look, what you saw, or what you think you saw…"

"I know what I saw. I have friends, you know. We'll find you. We'll find out where you live, and we'll hunt you down. You'll see." He scuttles off, pausing from time to time to look over his shoulder and point a knowing finger at me.

It's probably an empty threat. Probably. But his words echo Maxine's a little too closely for my liking. I continue to follow him at a more discreet distance.

I can bring the Change on myself if I want to, but I rarely do. I hate the way it disorientates me, warping my perception and senses. Every full moon I can feel my human-self and my snake-self bleeding into each other. I'm scared that one day I won't be able to Change back, or that I will wake up and find myself become some unholy hybrid, neither one thing nor another.

Or that I won't wake up at all.

But I have to do it this time. I tried staying in human form once when I was shedding my skin, just for kicks. It was bloody and excruciating. In snake form, it's almost pleasurable, like scratching an all-over-body itch.

I strip naked and stand in front of a full-length mirror, trying to see myself in snake form. It's a game I've played ever since my first Change, a game I never win, like trying to catch your reflection moving independently.

It always starts in the eyes. I watch the whites of my eyes turn black.

I'm crap at this. If Maxine were following the old man, she would be silent and virtually invisible, slipping through the shadows like smoke, no matter what form she was in. I stand out like dog's balls. When we were kids, she tried to teach me to move like she did. We even made up snake names for ourselves, calling each other Slither and Squeeze. But I could never get the hang of it. I think it was then we both realised that we could never be the same no matter how hard I tried, and the hate first got added to our love/hate mix.

The old man pretends he doesn't see me, leading me down a maze of side streets and alleyways until we come to a darkened dead-end behind a row of restaurants. Skip bins overflow with rotting vegetables and rancid meat. The man turns on me, snarling, his back to a wall and a knife in his hand.

I could easily run away. Adrenalin jolts my heart, making me gasp and pant. But before I even know what I'm doing, I've dashed the knife out of his grasp and clamped my hands around his throat. He falls backward onto the ground and takes me down with him.

He tries to fight back, flailing at my eyes with his filthy fingernails, but I have a longer reach than his. I pull my head away as if avoiding a bad smell, and his attack becomes more of a caress as his fingertips flutter against my neck. His eyes bulge and redden, his tongue protrudes, and his struggle becomes weaker. I press my knees into his chest to force the last gasps of breath from his lungs. It is over in minutes.

Somewhere in the back of my brain an impulse tells me that now, more than ever, would be a good time to run. But I stand over his still body for more perilous minutes, trying to sort out how I am feeling.

Not guilt. Not revulsion, although I should be nauseated at the sight of this bloody-eyed corpse, its head pillowed on a mound of slimy cabbage leaves, a foul dark stain seeping from its trousers. I feel...exhilarated. Omnipotent. And some kind of primal, visceral sensation that I have trouble identifying at first, it's so incongruous to the situation.

It is hunger.

The flight instinct finally wins out. I turn for home.

Lara tries to make me gorge myself a few days before each full moon to make sure I don't get hungry enough to escape and kill something when I'm a snake. I have to admit, she's saving me from deep unpleasantness; one time I came to after a Change to find myself throwing up a half-digested dog, and I'm not keen to repeat the experience.

She says she does it to protect innocent people, but that's a crock of shit. There's no such thing as innocent people. I think she's just afraid I will throttle her in her sleep.

She's not the only one. She's always going on about how hard done by she is having to be my keeper, that she never gets to have any kind of normal life. She has no idea what it's like to be me. One of these days she's going to piss me off once too often, and if I carry enough human anger over into my conscienceless animal state…well, I won't be held responsible for what happens then.

I like Maxine better when she is a snake. All of her human quirks and complexities are stripped away and she becomes a pure, simple creature of the earth.

And she is so beautiful. I can sit all night and watch her muscles work beneath her dappled skin, feel her power as she contracts and relaxes, coiling herself about my body. She likes to climb up me as if I am a tree trunk, although she has become too heavy for me to hold her up for long.

I don't want her to have the satisfaction of knowing that she was right, not yet, anyway, so I tell her while she is in the form of the beast. She won't understand now and won't remember later.

"I did as you asked, Maxine. I killed him."

She flicks her tongue, tasting the air in front of my face, and I stroke her head as if she were a cat.

"I won't do it again. Next time something like this happens, you're on your own."

It's an empty threat. Ours is the ultimate co-dependent relationship. Blood ties us together tighter than any promise.

And now that I've had a taste of killing, I might just volunteer for the job next time.

Something has changed in Lara. She is short-tempered and nervous, and has taken to chewing on her nails like she did when she was little, sucking the blood from her fingertips when she gets down to the quick. Like an over-anxious mother, I run through the possible causes in my mind—boyfriend trouble, drugs, that time of the month—and discount them each in turn. She won't tell me what's wrong, of course. That's the most annoying part of it. Usually she's only too eager to dump on me with all her problems, but just when I want her to talk, she clams up.

The full moon is still two days away. But, with strength I didn't know she had, she pushes me into my room and locks me in.

By the end of day two, I am ravenous.

When she finally lets me out again, I'm too hungry to have a go at her. I grab the peace offering from her hands—fried chicken and fries and a big bottle of coke—and fall on it without speaking. I'm halfway through it before I realise that she's not eating. She turns pale when I offer her some, and clutches at her distended belly. She retches and leans forward, bringing up her last meal on the floor.

Whatever she last ate, she had almost finished digesting it. All that remain are two little white summer sandals, the cheap plastic polished by stomach acid. They contain a pink pulpy mess that was once a pair of human feet.

All I can do is stare at the stuff on the floor. I want to throw up all over again, but my stomach is empty. Maxine drops her drink and it flows in a bubbly brown river to join the pile of vomit. "Oh my God, Lara, what happened? What did you do?"

"I don't know!" And it's true. The last couple of days are a blank. I remember sliding the bolts shut on Maxine's bedroom door, and then...next thing I know, I'm standing in a queue at some random fast food joint, feeling queasy and bloated and in a hurry to get back to Maxine.

"You Changed, didn't you?" Maxine accuses. "How...how could you? You can't Change. You have to stay human. You have to look after me."

Of course. It always comes back to her. Never mind what I might be going through.

I've never seen her so mad, and for someone who elevates rage to an art form, that's saying something. She seems to shimmer as her eyes darken, her body narrows and elongates and her legs fuse into one thick tube of scaly muscle. Still in mid-Change with her arms reaching out for me, she slides across the floor, moving impossibly fast for her size. She opens her mouth almost to a ninety-degree angle to expose her fangs. My perception lurches sideways, and I just manage to catch a glimpse of my own feet retracting into a serpentine tail before she slams into me.

We intertwine. She tightens and I flex until we are fused together like some living Gordian knot. Some detached part of my human brain tries and fails to remember which one of us was called Slither, and which one Squeeze.

Someone is screaming, but I can't tell whether it is her.
Or me.

Life In Miniature

Michael pulled his hoodie tighter around his face. A car was following him, he was sure of it. It was a little pale blue hatchback, a granny car with a dodgy fan belt by the sound of it, not the ominous quiet running black limo with black tinted windows that was supposed to follow lone walkers down darkened alleyways, but it made him nervous all the same. He fingered the switchblade in his pocket and walked faster, hunching over into the rain.

The car drew level with him and the passenger window slid down with a faint squeal.

"Do you want a lift?"

Michael stepped back from the curb. He'd seen the driver around, a thin woman in late middle age with grey-streaked straight dark hair. She liked to hang around the parks and overpasses, talking to the homeless kids, sometimes handing out money or food, all the time staring around with big, haunted looking dark brown eyes. Not a churchy do-gooder type—they always worked in pairs. Possibly an undercover cop, or more likely a guilt-ridden mother looking for her own runaway child. He dithered on the footpath, trying to second-guess what she wanted from him, what he could get from her, and what would be the cost.

"Are you hungry? You want to go get something to eat?"

It could be some kind of set up. But he was hungry. He was almost always hungry. He was also cold and wet. And she was a lone, unarmed, slightly built woman. He looked around, stepped from foot to foot and jiggled the switchblade.

"Yeah," he said, quietly, almost to himself, then louder, "Yeah. Yeah, OK."

Once inside the car, the woman held out her hand. "I'm Susan."

"Michael," he mumbled, shaking her hand awkwardly.

"I've seen you at the park, Michael," she said. "It must be very difficult for you, so young, living the way you do, no family…"

"You a cop or something?" His hand tightened on the door handle. The car had begun to pull away from the kerb, but if he jumped out now he might still escape without serious injury.

"No, nothing like that. I'm just…it worries me, seeing all these beautiful young people out on the street with nobody to care for them."

So that was her angle. Michael knew her type, but they were almost always men trolling for a bit of young rough. He looked at her more closely and shrugged. Could be worse.

As if reading his mind. Susan reached out and stroked the leg of his jeans.

"You're soaking wet," she said. "You'll get sick if you sit in those clothes for too long. I don't live far from here—you could take a bath while I wash and dry them for you."

"I wouldn't want to put you out…"

"It's no trouble," she said, far too quickly. No trouble at all."

Bingo. Hasn't been five minutes and already she's talking about getting me naked. He smiled and settled back to enjoy the ride.

Once inside her home, Susan was all business. Get changed in this room, put on this bath robe, give me your clothes, this way to the kitchen, are you allergic to anything? She left him alone perched on a stool at the kitchen bench eating a ham and cheese toasted sandwich and drinking hot chocolate. Just like mother used to make. The thought turned the food in his mouth to glue. Bored and nervous, he abandoned his half-eaten meal to explore.

He found two more bedrooms, none of them the master by the look of their spartan twin beds, then entered through an archway into what he guessed was a living room. He could just make out the shadowy outline of what appeared to be a very oddly shaped piece of furniture in the middle of the room. He flipped on the light switch.

"Holy shit."

Dollhouses weren't his thing, never had been and were never going to be, but he had to admit to himself, the sheer scale of the construction alone was impressive. The red tiled roof reached as high as his chin, and standing open on its hinges, the span must have been nearly ten feet. The house had four storeys with a miniature staircase zigzagging up at one end. The only other furniture in the room was a chair and long table against one wall, the table top strewn with an artisan's equipment—brushes, paint pots, sandpaper, scraps of wood and fabric, tiny screwdrivers, and other tools Michael could not identify. He drew closer to the house and bent to examine its contents.

It's like a 3D Cluedo mansion. One room taking up half of the ground floor must have been the ballroom, with its glossy polished wooden floorboards and tiny sparkling chandeliers. Another room on the second floor was clearly the billiards room, with toothpick-sized cues and perfectly spherical billiards smaller than baby peas. It even came complete with a replica of a bear skin rug, so realistic looking Michael half expected the snarling bear head to roar at him. A coverlet on a bed in a top floor bedroom that at first glance looked to be patterned in red polka dots was, on closer inspection, covered in a print of finely petalled roses. Miniature artworks in ornate gilt frames hung on the walls, all rendered in dizzying detail. Michael squatted on his haunches to inspect the ground floor kitchen. Copper cooking pots dangled on hooks from its ceiling, the smallest barely big enough to contain a single drop of water.

"What do you think?"

Michael started. Susan had slipped noiselessly into the room and stood behind him.

"It's...it's beautiful," he said.

"You really think so?" She smiled, her eyes liquid with tears. She reminded Michael of a puppy he'd once had that used to wag its tail even as it yelped in pain with every kick Michael's father had given to its ribs. He looked away from her, back to the house.

In one corner of the kitchen a tiny dog and a tiny cat squared off against each other. The cat's back was arched, its face creased in a snarl, its tail stiff and upright like a bottle brush. Michael ran his forefinger over the cat's back. The fur felt real, and strangely warm to the touch.

"Please don't touch anything," said Susan, pulling him back by the shoulder with a surprisingly strong grip. "They're very delicate, and break easily."

Michael murmured an apology. He frowned, peering into each room. Despite the intricacy of the house, there was something incomplete about it, something he couldn't quite put his finger on...

It was the dolls.

Little human-like figures populated it. They took up various positions of activity, some sitting, some standing, some sleeping. In contrast to the realism of the furniture, they appeared stiff and posed, as if their limbs had been forced and set in directions they did not want to go. The detail in their clothing was staggering: a little girl doll in the second-floor bathroom wore a hoodie similar to Michael's, and if he looked closely enough he could make out the individual teeth on the zipper—but there was something wrong with their faces.

They look...they look painted on.

In a different setting, their faces would have appeared acceptable, even skilfully rendered, but in such a realistic setting, they looked bland and unconvincing. Only one doll looked as if it belonged. In the top left-hand corner of the house a male doll lay in a bed, its body covered by bedclothes up to its chin. It had a prominent nose and its face was deeply lined, its expression one of deep-seated pain stoically borne. It looked so lifelike Michael almost thought he could see its chest rise. A blank-eyed female doll stood by the bed, leaning forward slightly as if about to press a hand to the male doll's forehead.

"That doll," Michael said, indicating the figure in the bed, "how come it looks so different from the others?"

"He looks like he is in pain, doesn't he? The man who...posed for me when I created that doll was on his death bed at the time. Normally I don't like them to look so unhappy, but it seemed appropriate for this setting, so I kept him as is. All the others..." Susan sighed. "I just can't seem to get them right. But I keep trying."

Michael stood. "This isn't for kids, is it?"

"They are my children," she said, nodding towards the house and flashing him a tight smile. She took hold of his elbow. "Come on, your bath is ready."

Michael half-expected to find a Hollywood-style hot tub overflowing with bubbles, but the bath was small and the water an odd, cloudy green colour. A pungent aroma wafted up to him on the steam. It reminded him at first of pine needles crushed underfoot, but with bitter, alcoholic undertones. He started to open the bathrobe.

"Are you going to join me?"

"No!" Susan backed away, her dark eyes huge with shock. "Oh, no, Michael, no, that's not...I mean, I didn't...I'll just leave you in peace." She paused at the doorway. "Just try to relax. It's important that you relax." Then she was gone.

Michael tested the water with his toe, then lowered himself gingerly into the bath. Try to relax, she had said. Easier said than done—strangely, the lack of sexual advances from Susan had made him more uncomfortable, not less. He leaned back and closed his eyes. How long had it been since he'd had a hot bath? He thought of Susan pressing her bony little naked body against his, the two of them lapped by the warm fragrant water, and his penis stiffened against his belly. He lifted a languid hand, then dropped it, suddenly too tired to masturbate. His erection subsided, and he did as he had been asked, drifting off into a state of semi-sleep.

He snapped awake with a sudden sense of panic. He had no idea how long he'd been out, but it must have been a while, because the water had become uncomfortably tepid. He sunk beneath the surface, taking in a lungful of water, and flailed back up, spluttering.

What the fuck was happening? He stretched his arms and legs out into a starfish shape. Susan must have drugged him and moved him in his sleep to a swimming pool or something, because he could not feel the sides or the bottom of the bath. He went under again, his mouth filling with water as he tried to yell for help. Something rubbery brushed against him, and he flinched away, only to feel it envelop him and lift him up. Susan's face, creased with worry, loomed above him. He shook his head like a dog shedding water. Whatever she'd slipped him had screwed with his perceptions; she looked impossibly huge, her arms stretching towards him encased in what looked like armpit-length yellow dish gloves. She raised a gargantuan, rubber-clad forefinger and stroked his face. Her voice stretched out deep and booming like a recording played at half speed.

"This doesn't hurt, I promise you. Please, Michael, just let go and relax. You're going to get stuck with that expression otherwise."

What—is the wind going to change? He giggled hysterically and tried to wriggle free from her grip, but his limbs had turned sluggish and refused to respond. She lifted him closer, closer, ever closer to her face, and his laughter twisted into screams.

Susan picked up the doll on her work bench and sighed. Yet another failure. She couldn't stand to work on them when they were naked, their bare skin against hers repulsed her, so using a magnifying glass and tweezers, she manoeuvred the doll into its tiny jeans, trainers and hoodie. With a little gentle manipulation, she would be able to massage its limbs into the pose she required, but as always, there was little she could do about its face. She put a finger under its chin and eased the mouth shut, but the look of terror still persisted in its wide eyes and taut cheeks. She picked up a piece of sandpaper and began to erase its facial features. Gently, gently now, don't want to flatten his profile out too much.

She held the doll as loosely as she could, but she could not escape feeling its heartbeat fluttering against her fingertips like a captive sparrow's.

The Witch's Library

Father's hands shook as he delivered the news.

"Children, you must know how loathe I am to do this, but I have withdrawn you both from school. Your mother and I..."

"She's not our mother." My brother spoke softly, but with a steely undercurrent belying his tender years. His hands clenched into fists at his sides.

It was as if Father had not heard him, his gaze rambling wildly, skimming over the spreading mildew stains on the ceiling, the peeling wallpaper, the broken window covered with sheets of yellowing newsprint, before settling on a point somewhere over my left shoulder. "...Your mother and I are too unwell to keep steady employment, so you must both work in our stead. Fortunately, I have secured you positions in my uncle's factory."

Father only had one factory-owning relative, our Great Uncle Gerhard. Gerhard visited us once a year at Christmas, bearing gifts befitting much younger children and hampers of exotic and overly rich foodstuffs that gave us stomach aches. I did not know what goods he produced, only that along with unwanted gifts, he brought the odour of soot, paint and chemicals, inadequately disguised with cologne and cigar smoke. Times had been hard across the city, and we had watched many classmates depart to work in the factories; the ones that returned alive were usually missing digits or eyes or entire limbs, or disfigured by fire or acid.

"You start tomorrow at 6 am," Father continued. "It is some distance to the factory, and I don't want you to get lost, so I'll take you there."

"Tell them they have to stay there for the week!" came the strident yet quavering voice of our stepmother, Valda, from the bedroom. I almost pitied her then; when Father first brought her home to meet us, her voice had been the prettiest thing about her, sweet and rich and enticing like an artisan-crafted torte, but whatever "medicines" she and my father had fallen prey to had degraded it. "Tell them they can come home on the weekend, but only if they bring all their wages."

"Ah yes, I almost forgot... Gerhard has a dormitory on site for his young workers. Like Valda says—work hard, be good, and save all your wages, and I will fetch you home later."

Hansel and I exchanged glances. Had it been just Father and us, we could have easily persuaded him to abandon this plan, if indeed he would have formulated it at all without Valda's incessant needling. But to argue further would only put Father under more stress and would ultimately be futile.

"Of course, Father." I tiptoed to kiss him on the cheek. "Whatever you think best."

We dined, if such a word could be applied to our paltry repast, on a watery and flavourless vegetable soup, of which Valda ate the lion's share, and copious cups of black tea. I forbore to eat it, pushing limp vegetables around in the grey broth. Father and Valda shook so much from their affliction that they could barely negotiate their spoons along the path from bowl to mouth. They retired early, and we went to our shared single bed soon after.

"What will we do, Hansel?" I whispered. "They say that once you start work in the factories, the only way out is through maiming or death, and I have no desire to experience either. And what of your scholarship to university? A mind such as yours must not be wasted in such toxic labour." Even at the age of thirteen, Hansel's genius had been pointed out to professors from the finest academy in the city, and he had a standing invitation to enter its halls free of charge once he was of age. I was no dunce myself in academic pursuits, but my intellect paled in comparison to my brother's.

Hansel stroked my hair. "Do not fear, Gretel," he said. I snuggled closer, the better to feel the comforting vibrations of his voice in his chest. "Where there is danger, there is always opportunity. I will find a way to bring us home safely."

Through the thin walls, I imagined I could hear the scratch and hiss of a match being struck alight and the bubble of melting narcotics. Father's and Valda's voices came to us, muted and incoherent, devolving into the animalistic sounds of lovemaking. They provided a curious counterpoint to the noises from the busy thoroughfare one storey below us; various vehicles, powered by steam or alchemy, hooted or chugged or fizzed along the street, and even at that hour, vendors still announced their wares in clamorous tones. We fell asleep in our chaste embrace to this profane lullaby.

Father shook us awake before dawn and bustled us out into the street with little discussion. He had shaken off his usual lethargy, taking long, loping strides with which we struggled to keep up, and tugging constantly at the hem of his jacket. I was almost grateful for the pace he set, for it went some way to warding off the cold.

I was unaccustomed to being abroad in the darkness; long, flickering shadows cast by the gas lamps disoriented me, giving the illusion that we were travelling beneath the branches of a chill and menacing forest. And Father took us on a route so circuitous that within the hour I was hopelessly lost. Hansel, however, took a keen interest in his surroundings, and more than once he paused on the pretext of tying his laces or removing a stone from his boots, all the better to more properly observe them. His lips moved almost imperceptibly as he recited a litany of directions to himself, thus committing them to memory.

However my mind's eye had pictured the façade of Great Uncle Gerhard's factory, the reality surpassed it in grotesqueness. It squatted on the outskirts of the city like a gargantuan toad of steel and stone. Chimneys and exhausts jutted haphazardly from the edifice and spewed forth clouds of noxious fumes. Father regarded it for a moment and sighed, a long, drawn-out sound that seemed to originate from the depths of his soul.

"My dear children," he murmured, each hand on one of our shoulders, "if there were any other way…"

Hansel shrugged off his hand and turned to face him. "Never mind, Father," he said with a trace of a sneer, "I'm sure Great Uncle Gerhard will take good care of us." And with that, he strode off, trailing me behind him.

The interior of the factory resembled a demonic kindergarten. Scores of thin and filthy children scurried over massive machines and constructions as if it were a playground, darting tiny hands in and out of furiously churning devices or deftly avoiding blasts of scalding steam. If it weren't for the looks of grim concentration on their faces, and the occasional whip-bearing adult lashing the backs of those who tarried at their work, it might have been all a big, risky game. The deafening noise of the machinery and the stench from the melange of chemicals overwhelmed my senses, and I swayed on my feet. Hansel steadied me with a hand under my elbow.

One sad-faced urchin led us to the overseer, a short man of middling years with a sparse beard and cruel eyes. He laughed when Hansel mentioned Great Uncle Gerhard, who was nowhere to be seen.

"If I had a penny for every child who told a similar tale, I wouldn't need to spend my days babysitting you snot-nosed brats," the overseer said. "Let's say you really are the Master's kin. If he cared about you, do you think he would put you to work in this hell hole?" A child a little younger than me scurried by, and the overseer snagged him by the collar of his shirt, causing him to stumble and choke.

"Arndt, take these two wretches to the dyeing vats and show them what to do. Mind that you show them well, or any mistakes they make will come out of your hide as well as theirs."

Arndt looked barely well enough to stand, let alone toil all day in a factory. His skin stretched too tightly over spindly limbs, and was patterned with burn scars in various stages of healing, many of which leaked a thick, yellowish discharge. The overseer released his grip on his collar. The boy did not speak, but jerked his head in a "follow me" gesture and set off with surprising speed through the labyrinth of machinery. It was all I could do to keep my footing and maintain the pace.

Arndt took us to the rear of the factory where a row of enormous vats sat atop furnaces into which several soot-stained children shovelled coal. Arndt clambered up a ladder at the side of the first vat and perched upon a broad wooden plank that ran over the vat's open mouth and extended from one side to the other. He beckoned impatiently for us to follow. We climbed up to join him, taking care not to touch the sides of the vat, which radiated a malevolent heat.

"This 'ere's what we call the *royal red*," Arndt explained, his sticklike legs dangling over the vat, "'Cos royalty is just about the only lot what can afford it. Once the cloth in here is dry and cured, the colour won't ever fade." He pointed down between his feet. Two giant paddles slowly churned the vat's contents. It looked like an immense tub of blood, the occasional fold of cloth brought into view by the paddles like pieces of flesh.

"But it's dead poisonous in this state, and you have to take care it's prepared right, else the first person to wear it will get awful sick. Your job is to watch the paddles, make sure they keep turning and don't jam up. If they do, take these…" He handed us each a long pole, the bottom two-thirds of which was stained crimson. "…And move the cloth around a bit. But *careful*, mind, 'cos you don't want it to tear. That's usually enough to get it moving again. If it ain't, you might have to give the cogs a bit of a clean out." He lay flat on the board and dangled his top half precariously over the edge, pointing at the exposed gears near the top of the thick metal rod to which the paddles were affixed. "You want to be quick while's you does it, 'cos if your fingers are still in there when it starts moving, you'll lose 'em. And the bosses don't want to see that kind of red in the mix." He smirked unkindly. "They must've liked the look of you two or somefink, 'cos this is what you'd call a plum post. Not much to do most of the time 'cept watch the red."

The board on which we sat vibrated gently from the paddles' movement. The odour that arose from the vat was pungent and unnatural, and made my head swim in a not entirely unpleasant way, and the gentle, repetitive swish of the paddles through the liquid was hypnotic. I teetered on the brink of the board, almost welcoming the compulsion to slip into the warm, vermillion waters below...

Arndt's gaze was sharp, his voice sharper, and it snapped me back to awareness with a jolt. "One more thing—whatever happens, *do not* fall in. Of all the ways to go in this place—and I've seen a few—that's the worst."

An angry shout rose up from the floor. Arndt cast an apprehensive glance at the foreman below, and without a further word, hastened down the ladder. Hansel kept a careful eye on the man's retreating back.

"We may no longer be attending school, sweet Gretel," Hansel said, "yet there is still the opportunity for a chemistry lesson. Did you notice the generous quantities of chemical substances stored about the factory?" I nodded.

"I recognize the symbols emblazoned on their containers," he continued, "although I wager most of the young workers here do not. Did you also notice that some are carefully stowed on opposite sides of the building? Why do you think that is?"

"I assume it is so there is little chance of them inadvertently coming in contact with each other."

"Well done, dear sister! You shall go to the top of the class. Now, if you will excuse me, I will take this opportunity while none of the supervisors are watching to go make some mischief." He pressed close to me and whispered in my ear. "When I return, do not hesitate—just take my hand and run." No sooner had he delivered his cryptic message than he was down the ladder and slipping amongst the machines.

I kept one eye on the vat beneath my feet as I tried to track Hansel's movements from my elevated vantage point, growing more and more apprehensive as I awaited his return. For the most part, he kept himself well hidden from the overseers, scooting across the factory floor behind their backs and ducking down behind barrels or boxes or bolts of cloth before they could turn. Every now and again he was not quite quick enough; then he would make a great show of lifting a box and moving purposely on an imaginary errand, and the man would turn his bored gaze elsewhere. He traversed the building, side-to-side and back-to-front and looping back on himself. To a casual observer his path would appear random and meaningless, but in his journey I sensed complexity and purpose.

The plank on which I sat bucked and shuddered, threatening to tip me into the toxic soup below. The paddles had become fouled with fabric, and strained against their bonds. I thrust the pole into the vat of dye and tried to untangle the snarl. Weighed down with liquid, the cloth was too heavy for me to shift, and I feared that if I put more of my body weight behind the pole, I might overbalance and fall to an untimely and gruesome death.

"Oi! You there! Put your back into it, you lazy slattern!" A supervisor stood at the bottom of the ladder and brandished a whip at me. "Don't make me come up there, or..."

His next words were drowned out by a booming explosion that set the board shaking anew. A great cloud of greenish smoke billowed up from near the factory's centre. Several smaller explosions followed in an almost synchronized fashion, and panicked cries and agonized wails filled the air. I prostrated myself upon the plank and buried my face in my hands.

A gentle tug on my ankle roused me from my terror-induced stupor.

"Gretel! Let's go!" It was Hansel, his voice muffled by a cloth wrapped about his nose and mouth as a makeshift filter. He tossed me a similar length of cloth and gestured to me to fasten it about my face, then gently encouraged me down the ladder. Even if the smoke were not too dense to see through, I was rendered virtually blind, the gases stinging my eyes until they watered uncontrollably. All about, foremen and workers coughed and retched and howled with pain, and the distinct crackle and heat of advancing flames menaced us. But Hansel's sense of direction was unerring as he led us through the devastation, out a service door, onto the street and into sweet, life-giving, fresh air.

"It was a horrible accident, Father. We were lucky to escape with our lives. And I fear that there is nothing left of Great Uncle Gerhard's factory." Hansel kept his eyes respectfully downcast, yet he turned his head slightly towards me and tipped a wink that Father could not see. In truth, we had not stayed long enough to see what had befallen the factory, but Hansel had assured me that the chain of chemical reactions he had set in motion would virtually guarantee its destruction.

After his initial surprise, Father was genuinely pleased and relieved to have us home again. Valda, of course, only had thoughts for the pecuniary loss of the earnings we could no longer provide. At first she raged, but soon fell silent, regarding us with acute speculation that was more intimidating than her wrath. I shuffled uncomfortably before her scrutiny, although it was not her attention that concerned me. Once we had escaped the factory and I had found myself whole and safe, my first impulse was to plunge back in to help the poor wretches still trapped inside, or at the very least alert the authorities to come to their assistance. But Hansel would have none of it.

"Were the positions reversed, would any of them have spared a thought for us? I think not," he had said. I had to concede that he was right, yet his callousness was disturbing, and the other children's fates weighed heavily on my conscience.

"Come, dear hearts," Father said, drawing us into an embrace. "We have little to offer for supper, but at least you will have a safe place to lay your heads tonight. Tomorrow we will set about finding you alternative employment."

"Yes," said Valda. "Yes, we shall."

It took Valda a day and a half to make good on her promise.

"I have secured you both a position with my former employers," she said. "There are no machines there, no dangerous substances, no inanimate objects that might hack off your limbs or poison your lungs." She spoke in a taunting, sing-songy voice, as if they were petty concerns that only cosseted babies might fear.

"No." Father's tone was flat, his arms folded firmly across his chest. "They will not go to that place." It was a rare show of fortitude on his part, and for a moment I saw him as I had when I was a very young child—as a hero, broad-shouldered and fearless and omnipotent. Hansel and I watched them take the measure of each other; I was equal parts intrigued at the unusual conflict and terrified at imagining the nature of Valda's former profession. After sending us to the horror that was Gerhard's factory, how heinous must this new place be if Father considered it worth defying his beloved Valda to save us from it?

Valda's lip curled. "And why not? It was good enough for you to go there, on more than one occasion. Or have you forgotten how we first met?"

"I have not forgotten," he said softly. "But this is different. They're just children." His voice held a hint of plaintiveness, and I sensed a minute giving of ground.

Valda snorted and waved a hand in dismissal. "Don't be ridiculous. They'll only be doing housekeeping duties—cooking and cleaning and suchlike, and running errands for Madam—at least, to start with. After all, they will not be children forever." The last words landed on Father like barbs; he flinched under their blow. Yet he remained unconsenting.

But our stepmother had one card left to play, and when I saw it fall from her hand, I knew our cause was lost. She slowly closed the gap between Father and herself, her hips swaying beneath her thin shift, then wound her bony body about his like a cat seeking affection. Slipping a hand under his shirt to caress his bare flesh, she stood on tiptoe to whisper in his ear. His mouth fell slack and his eyelids fluttered closed as if he were cast under the influence of a powerful mesmerist; I wondered, not for the first time, if she were not indeed secretly versed in the dark art of witchcraft.

"Very well," he said at last. "But it must only be temporary. As soon as we are able, we will fetch them back."

"Of course, my darling," she cooed. She turned, pressed her back to his belly and drew his arms about her like a cloak. In her triumphant smile we read the awful truth.

They would never bring us home.

This time Valda did not allow Father to escort us, but had them send a carriage to fetch us. It was an austerely elegant conveyance, its sleek lines devoid of windows and ornament and painted a glossy black, and was drawn by two equally glossy black horses. I had never seen live horses so close up; only the very wealthy kept them. With the almost metallic sheen of their coats and the plumes of vapour streaming from their flared nostrils, I could almost fancy them as elaborate automatons.

Valda had a hushed conversation with the carriage driver, a man of considerable stature who was dressed as plainly yet impeccably as his charges. He drew a small bundle wrapped in twine and brown paper from the inner folds of his coat and handed it to her.

"That evil bitch," Hansel growled, uncharacteristically obscene. "She's selling us!" He backed away, drawing me with him, but the driver lunged with surprising agility to grab us both by the arms. His massive hands easily encircled our biceps and held us as securely as iron cuffs.

"Oh no you don't, younglings," he said. "You now have a substantial debt to pay." He hoisted us both effortlessly into the carriage and slammed the door shut. The carriage rocked gently as the driver presumably took his seat at the front, and his soft *tsk tsk*, signalling the horses to walk on, filtered through the padded walls. The lurch of the carriage rolling forward took me unawares, and I fell to the floor. I was awash with panic, but Hansel merely leaned back against the soft, black velvet cushions and closed his eyes.

"Get some rest, Gretel," he said, "and save your strength for when we stop."

"You have a plan, I assume?" I asked. Eyes still closed, he nodded.

"And my only requirement in this plan is to run when you tell me?"

He opened one eye and gave me an impish grin. I sighed and picked myself up. All my life, Hansel had been my protector and saviour, my wisest counsel and my best friend. I had no reason to believe he would not prevail now. I did as he advised, even going so far as to recline on the seat. Despite my fear, the plush furnishings and the swaying, somnolent movement of the carriage soon sent me into a fitful slumber.

I had no idea how much time had elapsed when I awoke. The carriage had stopped, and a lifetime of compliance had me doing my best to rub the grit from my eyes and compose my hair and clothing into that befitting an obedient servant, despite the fact that Hansel and I had no intention of fulfilling our "obligations". We sat in anticipation for what seemed like an age until the door finally opened and we were hauled, blinking and disoriented, into the sunlight.

The driver had us again in his inexorable grip, and Hansel allowed him to propel us forward a few steps before he reached into his pocket with his free hand and cast what appeared to be a handful of scarlet dust into the man's face.

The driver's reaction was immediate; he let us go and clawed at his face with both hands, screaming in an incongruously high pitch. Hansel burst into a run, and I hitched up my skirts and set off after him. From somewhere close by came angry shouts and stampeding feet; something brushed at my back, a pursuer's grasping hand perhaps, and I yelped. Hansel slowed just enough to allow me to pass him, then threw another handful of dust over his shoulder. The irate yells gave way to cries of pain, then receded altogether as we left our would-be captors behind.

We ran like hunted rabbits, with no consideration for our whereabouts, our only thought to put distance between ourselves and an uncertain danger. We ran until I could run no further and my legs gave out underneath me, pitching me into the gutter where I retched with exhaustion. Hansel threw himself down beside me and huddled close, as much for his own comfort as for mine.

"Where are we?" I asked when I could finally draw adequate breath. Neither landmarks nor street signs looked familiar. The street on which we sat was narrow and ill lit, the cobbled road slippery with moss as if it were seldom used. Hansel looked around with wide-eyed bewilderment.

"I...I don't know," he finally said.

I could not recall another time when he had admitted to an absence of knowledge on any subject; of everything that had befallen us in recent days, this confession was the most frightening.

O ur headlong flight had worn through the last vestiges of leather on the soles of my boots, making me wince and limp with every step. Hansel's footwear had fared no better. Tired, cold, hungry and lost, we sagged against each other for support. We would have asked a passer-by for directions, but the quarters through which we staggered were oddly deserted. When we stepped out of the carriage, I had thought it no later than noon, yet dusk seemed to descend with unnatural rapidity; the neighbourhood was evidently too stingy for lamps, and darkness descended all too soon.

Then, just when I thought I could go no further, Hansel called out with joy.

"Look! A light!"

A few doors down, a warm glow emanated from a shopfront window. The light illuminated a sign that swayed enticingly from a multi-coloured awning. Painted on the sign in an amateurish yet enthusiastic style was the image of two children, a boy and a girl, with enraptured expressions, sitting side by side and reading from a book large enough to take up both their laps. The children bore an eerily close resemblance to Hansel and me.

It seemed so inviting, and we were so sorely in need of respite, yet as we drew level with the door, I hesitated. Surely the shopkeeper would tolerate us, two penniless ragamuffins, for no longer than a second before throwing us back onto the street...

With a cheery chorus of tinkling bells, the door flew open. A diminutive old woman, her grey hair pulled back into a dishevelled bun, peered up at us. Her face bloomed with creases as she smiled.

"My goodness, children! Whatever are you doing out alone on such a cold night? Come in, come in, you must come in!" She stood back to make way for us, beckoning vigorously. We all but fell through the doorway—and stopped abruptly in wonder.

It was a bookstore. A warm, glorious, light-filled bookstore. The abundant space was rendered intimate and maze-like with a multitude of shelves, all of which were crammed full with books. They overflowed onto the floor in dusty, teetering piles. I inhaled deeply, savouring the musty vanilla aroma.

"Sit, sit," the old woman said, waving a hand at a pair of overstuffed armchairs wedged into a corner. "You two look famished, you poor dears. I'll fetch us some tea and cake." She disappeared into the far reaches of the store.

I threw myself onto a chair as I had been bade; I barely had the energy to open my eyes, let alone explore the shelves, as intriguing as they were. But Hansel could not resist the lure of the books. He moved along one shelf as if in a trance, a forefinger caressing the spines as he mouthed the titles. Halfway along, he stopped and gasped. He stood stock-still and staring for several heartbeats, then with trembling hands lifted one particularly thick and ancient tome from its place and carried it with infinite care to sit beside me.

"Gretel, do you know what this is? It's an original treatise by Johannes Kepler, one of our most influential astronomers. It's exceedingly rare—there are rumoured to be only three copies left in existence." He lowered his voice and leaned closer to me, his eyes glittering with devilment. "They say that his mother was a witch, and that it was she who imparted to him knowledge of the stars." He opened the book and turned the yellow pages with a delicate hand, his mouth falling open in avaricious awe.

Somewhere towards the back of the store, a door slammed, and our hostess's jaunty humming could be heard as she made her way back. Hansel started and shut the book, sending up a cloud of dust, and concealed it beneath his coat. I opened my mouth to protest, but then the old woman was upon us, and the moment was lost. Hansel and I were reduced to trading baleful looks, mine silently exhorting him to return the book, and his warning me to hold my tongue.

"Don't be shy, children—eat up before it goes cold," the woman said as she pottered about pouring tea and buttering thick slices of an aromatic toasted fruit loaf. "You know, I get so few visitors, and my customers seldom care to stop and talk. They only want to make their purchases and rush off. So you do me a kindness by staying to humour a lonely old woman."

My instincts were at war with each other; one impulse told me to take Hansel by the hand and run before his theft was discovered, while another urged me to fill my empty belly with the delectable offerings before me. The latter won out, and I stuffed food and drink into my face as quickly as propriety would allow. Hansel also took the cup and saucer he was offered, and took several polite sips from his tea, but he held one arm pressed awkwardly against his side to keep the purloined book secure, while his gaze kept sliding towards the door.

"I thank you for your generosity, kind lady," he said, "but I fear we must depart. The hour is late, and we must get home—our father will be anxious for our return."

"Your father?" the woman inquired. She stood with her back to us, her posture suddenly tense and alert. "And what of your mother?" An innocent enough question, yet it seemed laden with portent.

"Our...our mother is..." I began. A lie was forming on the tip of my tongue, but the wayward organ became suddenly sluggish.

"Your mother is dead, isn't she?" The old woman turned around, the movement seeming to set the entire room spinning. The cup and saucer slipped from my nerveless fingers to shatter on the floor. Indifferent to my plight, she continued. "Perhaps if she were still alive, she might have taught you better than to steal from defenceless old ladies."

"I don't know what you're talking about," Hansel said brazenly. He tried to stand, but staggered and dropped back into the chair. The book fell from its hiding place, landing with a thump at the old woman's feet. Her lips curled into a mirthless smile.

"A thief *and* a liar," she said. "And a scholar to boot, judging by your choice of reading material." She nudged the book with her slippered foot. "My my, what an interesting fly I have caught in my web tonight." She studied Hansel for several long seconds, still bearing that unnerving smile, then approached him to take hold of his head, one hand beside each temple, and peer intently into his eyes. I tried to move, but a supernormal lassitude gripped my entire body; judging by Hansel's passivity and his glazed expression, he experienced the same phenomenon.

"Interesting," the old woman said. "Your mind...it is quite unlike any I have ever encountered before. You may be just what I need." She glanced at me with a look of disdain. "As for you— you'll only eat my food and prove yourself a general nuisance." From the folds of her apron she produced a wicked-looking carving knife and advanced on me.

"Wait!" Hansel's brow was beaded with sweat, his eyes wide with strain. "Whatever it is you want from me, if you harm so much as a hair on her head, you'll have none of it."

The witch—or that is what she must surely have been, given her uncanny influence over us—hesitated. "Ah, familial love... what a useless emotion! Mark my words, children, if you survive to escape these walls, you would be best advised to dispense with love entirely, as it will only be used against you."

If you survive... I shuddered in anticipation of the blade cleaving my throat. But the witch sheathed the knife and turned back to Hansel.

"Very well," she said. "I will not slay her...yet...but if you both value your lives, you will do what I say, to the letter."

We spent our first night huddled in a dark and dusty closet into which the old woman had dragged us whilst we were still incapacitated. Her name, we learned, was Rosine, and she set us to work immediately upon waking. My tasks, although tiring, were familiar and commonplace; I cooked, scoured pots and dishes, scrubbed floors, and dusted the rows of books that extended much further than the modest storefront suggested. With us as her captives, Rosine did not bother with the charade of opening the "store" to the public. In fact, although I explored every nook and cranny, I could find no trace of the store window or of the door through which we had entered. Besides kitchen and closet, there was only one other door in Rosine's library, and that was kept locked.

Hansel's purpose was more obscure. She kept him chained by the ankle to the wall, albeit with a comfortable armchair in which to sit, and I was ordered to keep him well fed and watered with whatever he desired, while I was only permitted the paltry scraps from her plate. Rosine brought him book after book on a wide range of arcane subjects, urging him to read far into the night and fuelling him with stimulating medicaments when exhaustion dragged his eyelids southwards. Her manner towards Hansel veered between extremes; one moment she spoke in gentle, cajoling tones that sickened me with their resemblance to Valda's manipulations. The next she stormed and raged and cursed, promising all manner of gruesome fates for us both if he did not master the texts. Hansel bore it all with equanimity, his only response to bend his head to the books in silence.

Rosine would not let me speak with Hansel, saying that I distracted him from his work while I neglected my own, so we were limited to brief, clandestine exchanges when opportunity arose. But I did not need him to confirm what my vision already told me; Rosine's books had enchanted him more thoroughly than any spell or elixir the witch could conjure. The eagerness with which he received each new tome was unfeigned, and his eyes shone with a fervour that bordered on madness. Many of the books contained obscure, long-forgotten languages, and from time to time I heard him quietly reciting the unfamiliar words in an urgent cadence that set the hairs rising on the back of my neck.

"What does she want of you?" I whispered, and his reply nearly stopped my heart.

"She wants me to summon the gods."

Hansel had discovered that the summoning ritual culminated in a human sacrifice, so he claimed a state of unreadiness to keep the witch waiting as long as he could, although I suspected it was as much to continue reading from the library as to prolong our lives. Rosine had been gathering her unholy texts for decades, attempting unsuccessfully to decipher them for just as long, and had searched for many years for the person with just the right paradoxical combination of brilliance and foolhardiness to interpret them for her; one might think that her solitary virtue of patience was well developed. Yet her state of agitation mounted exponentially by the day, until she could stand it no longer.

"The time is now!" she shrieked as she unfastened Hansel's chains. She grabbed us both by the hair, and with a strength surprising in such a frail looking woman, hauled us to the mysterious door, which now stood open at the top of a steep flight of stone steps. We were both too weak to mount much resistance as she lit a torch and pushed us before her. The steps descended into darkness to a seemingly impossible depth, the air growing colder and damper with each tread, and Rosine's flickering brand cast demonic shadows before us. I detected a hint of ocean brine, the stink of rotting seaweed and a spicy, more elusive odour not entirely in keeping with the scents of the sea.

At last we reached the bottom, where we slumped against icy stone walls and breathed great gulps of fetid air. Rosine took her torch to light several others mounted at regular intervals about the chamber in which we found ourselves. The flames revealed a frieze of symbols chiselled into the stone on three sides of the chamber. I did not know their meaning, but recognised some of the symbols from the books Hansel had been studying. On the fourth side, more stone steps went down into an underground lake, large and still and inky black.

Panting for breath with his head hanging low and skin pallid, Hansel looked close to collapse, yet the sight of the symbols seemed to invigorate him. Rosine twisted my hair in her fist and forced me to my knees. She drew her blade and pressed it against my throat.

"Say the words!" she screamed. "SAY THEM!"

She needn't have forced him; he had already begun, in a soft and low voice that gradually grew in intensity. Back in the library, the language had sounded forced and guttural, but here the words were in their natural element. Echoing off the walls, Hansel's voice was powerful and melodic, yet subtly ominous.

It was like listening to the call of giant, fantastical birds coming home to roost. He paced about the chamber like an actor upon a stage, his steps choreographed to music only he could hear.

The water in the lake began to move. It rippled at first from the centre outwards, as if struck by droplets of water from the unseen ceiling. A sound like the heartbeat of some huge creature insinuated itself into Hansel's chants, and as its volume rose, so too did the ripples, turning into waves that leapt higher and higher.

Then the first of the beings emerged.

They came one by one, snaggle-toothed or swarming with tentacles or domed all over with multi-faceted eyes. Some were small and agile, like an unholy hybrid of eel and ferret. Some were leviathans, dripping sediment from the ocean depths, their great domed heads hinting at an immense bulk concealed below the water's surface. And some defied all human perception of dimension and form, their very manifestation threatening to send me plunging irretrievably into insanity. They sang back to Hansel, these god-monsters, and the sound was like the torture of angels.

Rosine released me, dropped the knife, and stepped forward to descend the first few steps into the lake. She stood shin deep in the water, her arms wide in obsecration. The creatures paid her no mind; Hansel was their sole focus, and they swam and crawled and slithered towards him.

"Hansel! You must stop!" I struggled to make myself heard over the cacophony.

He turned to me, the torchlight distorting his features. In that moment, he was no longer my brother, but the god-monsters' kin. Then the illusion was gone, and I looked upon the face of a terrified boy.

"I can't!" he cried. "I MUST KNOW!" And he returned to his chant.

The ritual required a sacrifice, he had said. Very well, I thought grimly. They would have their blood—but it would not be ours. I picked up Rosine's abandoned knife and with all my strength, plunged it into her back. She stiffened and half-turned to claw at the spot where the knife entered her flesh, but she was not quite able to reach it. Uncomprehending, she looked up into my face. At the instant the awful understanding reached her consciousness, I pushed her into the lake.

The water churned with the feeding frenzy. I caught a flash of red, a glint of bone, a hank of grey hair whipping through the air, and I turned away. Hansel's face was frozen in a rictus of anguish; whatever I had done, it had not been according to the plan. Terror lent me strength, and I grabbed his hand to drag him up the interminable flight of stairs and into the library. With Rosine's enchantments broken by her death, we found the exit easily.

It led out onto the very street in which our home stood.

I wish that I could say that we lived happily ever after, but that is the province of fairy tales. In our absence, our guilt-ridden father had come to his senses and banished Valda. He was overjoyed to welcome us home, but never quite forgave himself for sending us away in the first place, and as a consequence held us both obsessively close until long after we reached adulthood.

Hansel never truly recovered. As we were leaving the library, he tried to take some of the books with him. He lacked the strength to resist when I forced him out empty-handed, and wept as if I were taking him to his death instead of away from it. He spent his first week of freedom in a delirium, and when he finally arose from his sick bed and went out onto the street, he found Rosine's library razed to the ground, its contents nothing but ash. Of the secret stairway and subterranean chamber, there was no trace.

Although I had ample opportunity, I never married. Instead, I became my brother's keeper, guarding him on his frequent visits to the ports where he was wont to stare into the sea and speak gibberish until the fishermen and stevedores threatened him bodily harm. Sometimes I felt the lure of the language myself, even although I did not understand it; it whispered to me in quiet moments of wakefulness and crept into my dreams. Rosine's words too came back to torment me—*you would be best advised to dispense with love entirely, as it will only be used against you.*

The god-monsters will return one day, of that I am sure. And when they do, I fear for humanity. The best I can hope for is that my bones have long been turned to dust before that day comes.

The Long Way Home

Timmo is always hungry. Food. Sex. Drugs. Booze. Attention. Shiny things behind glass that he has no hope of obtaining through legitimate means, that he covets fiercely even although they become as worthless as sand almost as soon as he has stolen them. Timmo has no innards, only a great, gaping hole of want that can never be filled.

Tonight, his most pressing hunger is for sex. And just like the shiny things, nobody is about to just hand it over. He will have to take it.

He knows just the spot in which to find it—a long, narrow pedestrian underpass that provides a shortcut between a train station and the relative safety of shops, schools and homes. The council won't install cameras or repair broken lighting because not enough people use it. And nobody wants to use it because it is ill lit and unsafe, an infamous hangout for flashers, drug dealers, and assorted other degenerates.

Tonight though, a storm rages above him. Water seeps and trickles down the walls, and pools in already damp, mossy patches. The weather will force a few commuters—the most foolhardy, desperate, and naïve ones—underground.

Timmo tucks himself behind a concrete pillar, concealed inside a patch of blackness, and waits. Soon, footsteps echo down the walkway, but he stays hidden; it sounds like two people, which would not be worth the effort. Just like the apex predator he pictures himself to be, he only targets the weak and the slow, the solitary straggler. Sure enough, two youths stroll past, unaware of his presence in the shadows, laughing and jostling each other over some private joke. The next passer-by is a lone male, tall and broad-shouldered with a don't-mess-with-me look in his eye and swagger in his step, and he too goes unmolested.

Then the underpass is once again deserted, except for Timmo. He'll probably have to wait now for the next train, he thinks. The odour permeating the underpass—mildew, piss, the faint whiff of a small, dead creature trapped and decaying—seeps into his skin. The minutes pass sluggishly. He slips his hands inside the waistband of his track pants and desultorily masturbates; when it happens, he will need to be ready. Perhaps it's the anticipation, or perhaps it's some quirk caused by the weather, but the air feels charged with menace. It is the feeling of getting caught out in the open in a lightning storm, of being trapped in the middle of a large, agitated crowd that is tipping into riot, of looking helplessly through a car windscreen as the world tumbles, over and over and over...

The hair on the back of his neck stands up, and his heart races faster than it should, even allowing for the drugs in his system. He takes his hand off his semi-erect penis and reaches instead for the box cutter in his pocket. Someone is coming, the footsteps sounding muted and tentative, almost as if the walker is on tiptoe. Timmo chances a look.

The lone pedestrian is looking back over one shoulder, and so swaddled against the cold, he can't tell at first if they are male or female. Then the head turns, revealing a pale, moon-like face and wide, frightened eyes. It is a woman, a little older and fatter than he prefers, but what was that thing his father used to say? *You don't look at the mantelpiece while you're stoking the fire.* He thumbs open the blade on the box cutter and draws back into the dark.

The woman advances slowly at first, her pace increasing the closer she gets to the exit at the other end. As she draws level with his hiding place, Timmo reaches out and grabs her. He has to act quickly—slam her up against the wall to knock the wind out of her before she has a chance to scream, and put the blade to her throat to secure her continued silence.

"Make a sound and I'll kill you," he whispers, pricking her

skin with the point of the blade. The threat draws a few drops of blood, and fat, quiet, ugly tears. Both predator and prey are panting from the adrenaline, their breath mingling, the moment oddly intimate. He presses her hard against the damp wall. It's impossible to tell what her body might be like underneath all those layers of clothes, and for a moment he regrets the decision to go out in such shitty weather; it's going to be a bitch getting enough of her uncovered to reach the sweet spot. Nevertheless, he makes a start, fumbling open her coat and delving one-handed under a sweatshirt, T-shirt and singlet to find the fastening on her jeans.

"Wait, wait, wait!" the woman whispers back. If she only moved as fast as she talks, Timmo thinks, he would never have caught her. "You don't really want me, do you? Not when you could have...her." She jerks her head in the direction from which she came, and sure enough, he hears it; the unmistakeable clicking sound of stiletto heels.

He keeps the blade in position as he leans around the pillar to check out the newcomer. She walks slowly while holding a dripping umbrella in one hand and looking intently down at the phone in her other. The light shining from the screen reveals a pretty woman in her twenties, of Indian descent at Timmo's guess. A heavy, black overcoat swings carelessly open over tailored business attire that accentuates a slim figure and gym-toned legs. She is everything Timmo desires and loathes. And here she comes strolling through the underpass like she owns the place, completely ignorant of the danger.

Clip. Clop. Clip, Clop. Clip, clop.

He returns his attention to his current captive. "If you warn her, or if you call the cops, you're both dead," he murmurs in her ear. It is an empty threat, but he is well-versed in the art of intimidation; her only immediate thought will be of putting as much distance between them as possible, and by the time she slows down enough to think clearly, it will be too late. He hauls her away from the wall and gives her a little shove to propel her on her way. She takes off as fast as her chunky frame allows. Timmo's new quarry stops, looks up, frowns, glances towards the darkness where Timmo lurks, then back after the other woman, of whom nothing remains but the fading sound of practical shoes clomping rapidly on pavement. She continues walking, but even slower now, the phone stowed in her pocket and the umbrella ever-so-slightly raised.

"Hello?" she calls, and winces as the sound reverberates in the concrete tunnel. In the dark, Timmo smirks. When she is nearly level with him, he steps out, still smirking, and blocks her way. There's a hint of fear in her dark eyes, but mostly her expression is one of annoyance. Bitch didn't even flinch, he thinks, and hates her even more as she stands her ground and imperiously tilts her chin upward. She hasn't noticed the box cutter, so he brings it up between them.

And...*there. There is the fear.*

They stand frozen for several moments, she staring at the blade, he staring down the front of her crisp, white blouse, each trying to anticipate the other's next move.

"Hey! Do you guys wanna party?" The words are slurred, the voice young and feminine, and they both turn to look at the caller.

It's a girl not quite out of her teens, risking hypothermia in butt-hugging denim shorts and a crop top, teetering into view, her unsteady gait no doubt due to more than the ludicrously high stripper heels she wears. She is too far away for Timmo to see her eyes, but he imagines that her pupils must be wide, wide, wide.

Now, that's *what I call an easy meal.*

The businesswoman has a strange look on her face as she stares at the other girl, almost as if she sees a different creature entirely. Something passes between the two women—an infinitesimal nod of recognition, or a more detailed communication coached in an arcane, feminine language—and is gone, leaving Timmo to question whether he really saw anything at all.

"Awww, baby, you don't wanna bother with her, now do you? I bet I could show you a better time." The girl is closer now, close enough for Timmo to revise his initial estimate of her age down a few years. Might be she's not even legal, he thinks, and this suspicion obscurely bothers him; it's not like he makes a habit of concerning himself with matters of right or wrong, yet there are lines even he won't cross.

Yet his cock has other ideas. It throbs, painfully and insistently, no longer in need of manual stimulus. The girl is within his reach now, near enough that he can smell her perfume: a synthetic approximation of roses, a touch of days-old patchouli, and an incongruous hint of sulphur. He is so intent on her, he doesn't even notice the other woman sidling around him and away.

The girl's hair hangs in two long, dark braids on either side of her face, reinforcing her childlike appearance. Also childlike is her ignorance of how much danger she is in. She tilts her head and smiles at him. *That smile…*

Timmo feels suddenly woozy. The atmosphere of impending doom intensifies. He sways on his feet and blinks rapidly. He takes a step back, all the better to refocus and have a good, long look at her.

He was mistaken. She is a child, not even ten years old, dressed in her mother's clothes. She is flat-chested and spindly-legged, and her eyes are moist with an unspoken plea to *please don't hurt me…*

No, that's just a trick of the light. How could he have not noticed this before? She is fully grown and heavily pregnant, a fertility goddess whose swollen belly undulates with the movements of an unborn child not wholly human…

No. She is a hunter, not clad in denim and lycra but in the pelts of her prey. Grisly trophies sliced from her human victims dangle from her belt, and the knives she holds in both hands still drip with blood…

And her eyes are blue. No, they are brown, dark brown, almost black. No, they are yellow, and her pupils are vertical, like a cat or a snake…

"What's that in your hand?" Her voice is controlled and silken, all traces of slurring gone. Timmo looks down, aware for the first time in what feels like aeons that he still holds the box cutter. "Here, let me take that before you hurt yourself." She plucks the weapon from limp fingers and hurls it over his head. Somewhere far from his grasp, it clatters on the ground, then goes quiet.

The girl smiles, and smiles, and the smile becomes a chasm,

and the chasm is lined with sharp, sharp teeth. And yet there is a part of Timmo's brain that can't accept he's lost control of the situation. Even as she lifts those blood-drenched knives, even as the knives grow and lengthen into scimitars, even as she spins and whirls her swords before him in a deadly dance, he thinks—

She should be afraid. Why is she not afraid?

The man would not normally brave the underpass, not at night anyway, but he did not come prepared for such foul weather. He is five steps into the tunnel when he hears a scream. It is so filled with agony and terror that he cannot tell if it is human or animal.

A brave man would continue into the tunnel to rescue or help the poor creature. A conscientious man would call the police. But this man is no hero—he is merely cold, tired and hungry. He turns back to take the long way home, and hunches into the rain.

Late for Eisheth

I should never have become a psychotherapist. Ask any of my peers why they took up the profession, and they'll spout the party line—"I just want to help people." Puh-lease. I went into it for a whole host of reasons, but that ain't one of them. Mostly, I did it because I love to know everybody's dirty little secrets...the dirtier, the better.

Problem is, most people's secrets are banal and boring. My wife doesn't understand me, blah blah blah. I wet the bed until I was in high school, blah blah blah. I like to wear women's clothing, blah blah blah. My uncle abused me when I was ten, blah blah blah. Sometimes I have dreams that I'm fucking a goat, blah blah blah. After a while, they all start to blur into one.

I used to think that I was pretty good at faking sincerity, but word must have got around that I'm a crappy therapist; I guess there are only so many scripts you can write for anti-depressants before your patients get wise to you. My practice has been dwindling steadily over the past few months, so Reason Number Two—the money—isn't stacking up anymore either.

So, I'm daydreaming about an alternative profession (Race-horse owner? Professional gambler? Hitman?) when Joe and Glenda Henry show up for their 4 pm appointment. Precisely on time. Perhaps I could tick the box marked "Obsessive Compulsive" for at least one of them and fob them off with that diagnosis for a few sessions. They're an unremarkable-looking couple, late fifties at a guess, dressed in drab, shapeless clothes that inadequately conceal drab, shapeless bodies. Joe looks like he's afflicted with more than just a naturally aging body and an indifferent lifestyle; his skin has an unhealthy grey hue to it, and he carries himself with a certain delicacy, as if he is in constant pain. I don't hold out much hope that these two will provide much in the way of entertainment value.

"And what can I do for you today?" I say, plastering on my best professional smile.

Glenda looks down at her lap and twists the hem of her blouse. "Mr Peterson..."

"Please. Call me Adam."

"Okay, Adam," she says tentatively, rolling my name around her mouth as if it is a new and not entirely welcome flavour. "My husband...Joe...has been unfaithful." I resist the temptation to roll my eyes; of course he has. That's what brings most couples to my office. Although boring old Joe doesn't look like he has it in him. I start to wonder if they are wealthier than they look—money can be a powerful aphrodisiac—and I sit forward a little in my chair.

"He's been visiting a pr- pr- pr...prostitute!" she finally gets out, and bursts into tears. I push a box of tissues across the table towards her. Joe has the grace to look embarrassed, and ineffectually pats his wife's shoulder as she sobs into her hands. She looks up at me, eyes red.

"He shouldn't even be able to have sex!" she wails. "He has prostate cancer, and the treatment's made him impotent. I just don't understand where it's all gone wrong!"

Or maybe he just told you he was impotent because he doesn't want to fuck you, I think. I look to Joe, inviting him to tell his side of the story.

"It's...ummm...complicated," Joe says. "I love Glenda, truly I do, and never wanted to hurt her, but this woman...if you saw her, you'd understand." His pathetic puppy-dog eyes beg me to empathise, man to man. Beside him, Glenda ramps up the hysterics.

"Don't worry," I say. "You've come to the right place. 90% of marriages affected by infidelity will survive if the couples commit to therapy." It's a bullshit statistic, but I need the cash, and I figured that if Joe has the funds to splash around on whores, the least he can do is send a little my way. After all, am I not a whore myself, of a kind? Paid to feign emotion and look like I give a shit.

"I'll need to see you both separately before your next couple's session," I say as I write out a couple of prescriptions. "In the meantime, I'm starting you both on a course of anti-depressants."

"Are you sure that's necessary?" asks Glenda. "It might interfere with Joe's other medications, and I was hoping that…"

"Oh, yes," I say, smiling wide enough to hurt. "Trust me, I'm a doctor."

Joe is the first to attend his solo session.

"You can't make me stop seeing her, you know," he says, his chin jutting forward in what I guess is a rare show of defiance. "Nobody can. "

I hold up my hands in a calming gesture. "It's OK," I say. "I'm not in the business of making people do things against their will. That's what wives are for, isn't it?"

He looks at me blankly; so much for using humour to put the patient at ease. I try another tack.

"Tell me about this woman."

"I've been seeing her for longer than Glenda thinks—since before my cancer diagnosis, in fact. It's true, the treatment does make me impotent. At least, when I'm not around Eisheth, it does. That's her name—Eisheth."

Funny name, I think. What's wrong with good, solid, traditional hooker names like Bambi or Divine or Lola?

"That's the thing," Joe continues. "This cancer, it's killing me, I know it is, but when I'm with Eisheth…"

"You feel alive," I finish for him, and stifle a yawn; I've heard this story before.

"Yes!" he says delightedly. "So you do understand!" Not really, but I let him think I do.

"So…how did a supposedly happily married man come to be engaging the services of a sex worker?" I say. "Were you really as happy as you say you were, or do you think perhaps your actions were a subconscious cry for help?"

Joe isn't even listening to me properly. He's leaning back in his seat with a faraway look in his eye, smiling faintly. Evidently he is recalling the magical moment when he first met his beloved Eisheth. I sigh and settle back too; it looks like this is going to be a long story.

"I first met her when I was coming home from a work function. Glenda had stayed home with a migraine, and I wanted to get back to her as soon as I could. She gets nervous when she's home alone. Anyway, the restaurant had been in an unfamiliar part of town, and I got myself turned around a little trying to make my way home. I found myself amongst all these small factories and warehouses…light industrial, you know what I mean. The streets were deserted because it was nearing midnight, so when this woman suddenly stepped out of a doorway, well, I must admit I was a little startled.

"She was dressed unusually, like she'd been at a toga party or something, in this thin, draping fabric," —he makes vague gestures about his body—"with a braided gold belt around her waist. Her dress was white. Pure. Virginal." He smiles in fond remembrance, and I suppress a smirk.

"It was that white dress that startled me, you see—for a second I thought she was a ghost." He chuckles at his own superstition. "It was far too flimsy for the weather, and she was barefoot, so I stopped to ask her if she needed any help."

"Like any true gentleman would," I supply. The irony is lost on him; he nods fervently.

"She approached the car," he says, "and that's when I saw them."

"Them?"

"The other women. Three of them, and all dressed the same way. And the man."

"Their pimp?"

Joe grimaces. "That's such an ugly word. No, Eisheth said that he was her husband, and the other women his wives."

Okay, now it's starting to get interesting.

"So what are we talking here? Some extremist Mormon cult

low on funds? You did say that she was a prostitute, right?"

"Not just any prostitute," he says, his eyes shining with creepy fervour. "A holy prostitute. You know, like they used to have in ancient Greece. Making love to honour the gods."

"And exchanging money for it."

"Yes. That's an essential part of the ritual, Eisheth said. I didn't have to pay much—I only had twenty dollars in my wallet, and that sufficed, so long as I was crossing her palm with metaphorical silver."

I whistle. "Twenty dollars…listen, Joe, I hope you used a condom, because that sounds extraordinarily cheap. As in, disease-ridden cheap…"

He laughs. It is an oddly depressing sound. "You don't know the half of it." He leans in to me and whispers, even although there is nobody else around to hear him.

"I think she gave me prostate cancer."

"Umm… I'm not a medical doctor, but I'm pretty sure that cancer isn't contagious."

Joe's eyes brim with tears. "I tried to say no. Told her I wasn't that kind of guy, and that I had a wife waiting for me at home. But she was just so beautiful… Afterwards, I promised myself that it was a one-time mistake, and that I'd walk away from it like it never happened. But two nights later, I was back there again. I just couldn't help myself. It was like I'd been hypnotised.

"It's too late for me now, Adam. She's dug her claws in me, and I can't get away. I mean, actually dug her claws in me." In one surprisingly swift movement, he hauls his sweater and his T-shirt over his head and turns to show me his pale, flabby back. It is a pus-ridden mess of scars, both fresh and faded. I choke down the gorge that rises to the back of my throat. The plot has definitely thickened; that is one serious S&M fetish, and I'm willing to bet that dear, sweet Glenda doesn't know about it.

As if reading my mind, Joe says, "Tell Glenda when she comes for her session to hang in there. She doesn't know it yet, but I haven't got long to live. At least this way she'll still get the insurance payout." He stands and leaves the office, a beaten man in all senses of the word.

Unlike Joe, Glenda seems to have grown a backbone since I saw her last.

"I want Joe committed to a mental institution," she says.

"On what grounds?"

"For his own safety and protection. That...that..." Her upper lip curls, and I have the disturbing mental image of a feral dog about to attack. "That slut that he's been seeing," she spits, "is a monster."

Okay, so maybe she does know about Joe's kink. "Listen, Glenda," I say soothingly, "human sexuality is extraordinarily complex. There's a huge spectrum of what can clinically be considered normal, and unless Joe's life is in danger or he's being forced into something against his will, then I'm afraid..."

"No, no, no! I mean she's an actual monster. With claws and fangs and a real fucking forked tail!"

I don't know which is more shocking, Glenda's lunatic revelation or the fact that she dropped the F-bomb. I offer her a glass of water, a diversionary tactic while I think of a response.

"What makes you think she's a monster, Glenda?" I say, once I've picked my jaw up off the floor.

"I wanted to find out what I was up against, so a few days ago, I followed him. I know that when he's going to see her, he leaves the house around 11:30 pm. That's how I found out about her in the first place; most nights I'm fast asleep at that time, and he's able to get out and back without my knowing, but this one time I woke up with a stomach upset... Anyway, I told Joe I was going to stay at a friend's house for a few nights, but instead I staged a stake out. Parked my car a few streets down and waited until he drove past, then trailed him just like they do in the movies." She sounds very proud of herself, so I don't have the heart to tell her—yet—that in my professional opinion, she's a crazy psycho bitch.

"I watched where he parked his car, then went a little further on and stopped out of sight, then doubled back on foot. They were there, alright...four of them, dressed in white, and with the hottest looking man I've ever seen in my life. Joe wasn't their only client—there were blokes coming from all sides, lining up to hand over their money, and they were looking at these… things…like they were Angelina Jolie and Cleopatra and Helen of Troy all rolled into one. But I could see their true likenesses.

"Sure, they all had pretty faces and big, perky breasts, like you'd expect a hooker to look. But they all had talons too, massive ones, like bear claws." She holds her hands apart to demonstrate the length. "A couple of them had horns sprouting from their temples. One had little horns, and the other had big spiralling ones like a ram's. One had clawed feet, like a vulture's. And Eisheth, the one that Joe went to…she had a tail. Long and thick, with a fleshy little fork at the end of it, which she used to put down Joe's pants and…"

For a moment I think she's going to start crying again, but no; by the look on her face, she's rendered momentarily speechless by blind fucking rage.

"He handed over some money, and then they did it, right there in the street! And all the while the other three whores were servicing their clients too, giving them hand jobs and blow jobs and I-don't-even-know-what-you-call-it-jobs, and sometimes even taking on two or three men at a time. There weren't just having sex with these men, either—by the time they'd finished, it looked like a mass murder crime scene, what with all the blood from the biting and the scratching. I don't know how some of those men managed to walk out of there. I stayed hidden until it was all over and the men had left, and then…well, the next part is the worst.

"Remember the gorgeous man I mentioned earlier? Well, he stripped naked, and the women all went to him literally dripping with semen, and they kind of…" She wrinkles her nose in disgust. "Well, it looked like they were depositing it on him, or in him, or…I don't know. It was all hands and mouths and cunts and arseholes, going up and down on his massive, throbbing…"

By now I don't know whether to be aroused or repulsed, so I go for a bit of both, tucking my chair in a little more snugly under my desk to hide my growing erection and taking several gulps of water from the glass I'd offered Glenda.

"And then?" I manage to squeak. Glenda heaves a big sigh and looks out the window for a moment before replying.

"I suppose I may as well tell you," she says. "It's not like I have any dignity left. When the women had finished servicing him, I came out of my hiding place and approached him. I had nearly one hundred dollars in my wallet, and I'd seen an ATM a couple of streets away if that wasn't enough. I couldn't even remember the last time Joe and I had had sex, and I was so mad at him, I would have slept with damn near anybody just to get revenge. And this man was so handsome, and I thought…I hoped that if I offered him enough money, he just might…"

"Did he?" I ask, although I'm not sure that I really want to know the answer.

"No," she says in a voice barely above a whisper. "He said that only his wives take payment, and that twenty years ago he would have gladly obliged me, but now…now I'm too old."

As shaken and stirred as I am by this fresh confession, I can't help but parrot my usual schtick. "Age needn't be a barrier to a satisfying sex life…"

She cuts me off with a wave of her hand. "Save it, Adam," she says. "Are you going to help Joe or not?"

I pretend to give her question serious thought. "It's not that simple, Glenda," I say. "I'm not saying that I don't believe you, but the Medical Board would require me to state that Joe is a risk to himself in his compromised medical state. And in order to do that, I'll have to witness this…abuse first hand."

Glenda falls for it hook, line and sinker. She snatches up a pen and notepad off my desk and scribbles something down, then tosses the notepad to me.

"Here's the address."

I can see why Joe neglected to mention the tail. I almost don't notice it myself, I'm so fixated on that perfect set of big, high, round tits. The nipples, teased hard by the chill midnight air, are clearly visible through the translucent white fabric of her gown. She approaches me, smiling slightly, and it's like she's moving in slow motion, every sway of her hips imprinting on my brain. Her tail swings languidly from side to side, and I wonder where she gets such realistic looking props. Tail Lady is flanked by three other equally well-stacked friends, so it looks like I'm going to have a choice of delights. Usually I prefer to watch high level kink rather than participate in it, but I'm here now, so...

"And you are...?" she asks.

"Adam," I murmur, eyes fixed on her chest. She gives off a faint odour of stale sex and sulphur, a scent that I find strangely arousing.

"Did you say Adam?" says the ravishing brunette on her right. "My first husband's name was Adam. He was a complete tool." With that, she turns her perfect nose up in the air and stalks off in search of more appropriately named clientele.

"Don't mind Lilith," Tail Lady says. "She gets a little sensitive sometimes." She extends her hand, and I shake it, marvelling at the silky texture of her cool skin. "Now, Adam, what brings you here this evening?" Her smile says she knows exactly what I have come for, and that she can't wait to get down to business.

"Umm...Joe sent me."

"Did Joe tell you the price?" she says.

"Ah, yeah, he said you were...inexpensive."

"Inexpensive?" She laughs, and the sound makes my cock throb painfully. "Well, I suppose if you value it so little..." I have a vague sense that we are talking about two different things; nevertheless, I take a twenty dollar bill out of my pocket and hand it to her.

In an instant, she is on me; she hauls my pants to my knees, hitches her skirt up around her waist, and with an extravagant sigh, slides herself down on my cock.

There's another thing that Joe forgot to mention. It hurts.

Entering Eisheth is like plunging into a bath of ice water. I try to pull out, but I'm stuck fast. My teeth begin to chatter with the cold, and Eisheth stills them with her mouth clamped over mine. Her teeth are unnaturally sharp, and they pierce my lips. Blood intermingles with spit and trickles down our chins. Mercifully, her talons are embedded in the brick wall at my back, but her prehensile tail roams over my body, delivering stinging little slaps wherever it finds bare flesh. She inhales, and it feels like she is vacuuming my guts out of my body.

I come harder than I ever have in my life.

She drops me unceremoniously on the pavement and I slump to the ground, too drained to move. I lie there for a while, gathering my strength, watching Eisheth and her equally freakish colleagues go to work on their other clients who are shuffling zombie-like from the shadows. One poor bastard turns up in a wheelchair with an oxygen tank on the back, and Eisheth flicks on his parking brake and straddles him in the chair. Presiding over it all is their pimp, an unreasonably tall, blue-eyed blond Adonis dressed in a midnight blue suit tailored so sharply you could cut yourself on it. Smarmy-looking prick is so handsome, he doesn't seem real.

Maybe he's not real. Maybe Eisheth slipped some hallucinogenic drug into my mouth when she was damn near chewing my face off. Maybe I'm imagining everything. I giggle. I'll just close my eyes for a little while, and when I open them again, this will all be over.

I get a message on my phone from a disturbingly jubilant Glenda. Joe is dead. The funeral was a small affair for family only, but I'm welcome to attend the memorial service next Tuesday if I want. Oh, and I can cancel all future appointments for her as well as Joe. Apparently, the money she would have spent on therapy is going to be better served taking herself on a holiday to Kenya.

No matter. I can manage without a client or two. My visits to Eisheth cost little (last week I paid her with a digital watch with a flat battery, the week before it was a handful of coins I'd found down the back of the couch and a used bus ticket), and truth be told, these days I have fuck-all energy to deal with clients anyway.

I check the clock. 11:23 pm—nearly time to leave. I give myself the once-over in the bathroom mirror before I go. Not that it makes any difference to Eisheth; she'd fuck me if I was dipped in pig shit and rolled in broken glass. The shadows under my eyes are getting so dark, it's starting to look like someone has punched me repeatedly in the face. I grimace at my reflection and check out my teeth. My gums have been bleeding a little lately, and some of my teeth feel loose in my mouth, a fact that probably should worry me but somehow doesn't.

I go into a coughing fit and spit up blood into the sink. I go off into a trance for a few minutes, staring at it and thinking how the spray pattern and the contrast of the bright red colour against the white porcelain of the sink is almost pretty. Then I come around.

I wouldn't want to be late for Eisheth.

Symbols of Damnation

The customer wears a silver crucifix around her neck. Felix tries not to look at it, tries to focus on a point somewhere above her left eyebrow, but he knows it's there, and his gaze is drawn inexorably back to it. It's only tiny, he tells himself, you can barely even make out the detail on it, let his eyes lose focus a little and it could be any old pendant... But it doesn't work. He rubs the sweat off his palms onto his jeans, surreptitiously at first but then with more rhythm and force, as if the repetitive motion will distract him from the sickening thing resting on the woman's chest. His supervisor Belinda glances sideways at him and frowns.

"Felix, are you...?"

He closes his eyes, thinks instead of his new girlfriend Harmony. Harmony would never wear a crucifix. Harmony is an atheist, an anarchist, and a whole heap of other "ists" that are antithetical to organised religion and its symbols of damnation. He pictures her naked, unadorned breasts, her blaspheming, lascivious pierced tongue, her black-lacquered nails digging into his back, and smiles to himself; he could be falling in love.

A loud thump on the counter snaps him out of his fantasy, and he opens his eyes. The customer has leaned forward, and the crucifix is now mere inches away. It is all he can do to stifle a yelp.

"Have you listened to a word I've said?" the woman yells. "What are you, some kind of retard or something? I'm telling you, this fucking phone doesn't work!" Other customers turn around and stare at them both. "Where's your manager? I want to speak to the manager!"

Belinda excuses herself from the customer she is dealing with and slides in front of Felix, making calming gestures at the woman with one hand and waving Felix away with the other. She shoots him a furious look and mouths at him over her shoulder. *Out the back. Now.*

Obediently, gratefully, he goes, sits at the tiny cluttered desk in the store's closet-sized office, tries to settle his ragged breathing, and dabs at the tears forming in the corners of his eyes.

"**W**atch Felix for me, Clare," Mum says. "Make sure he doesn't get into any mischief." She walks off to speak to Father Albert before the service.

Mum told him that Dad is in the big box at the front of the church. Felix eyes the box nervously; any minute now, he thinks, his father is going to jump out of the box and give him a big fright. He usually likes coming to church. It's pretty. It's especially pretty today, with all the flowers around Dad's box, but nobody else seems to be having a good time.

He climbs up onto a pew, puts his thumb in his mouth and drums his heels on the wooden boards. He looks at his favourite part of the church, the big stained-glass window showing the Virgin Mary and a toddler-sized young Jesus. Clare sits beside him, her bloodless lips pressed tightly together.

"Stop that," she says, yanking his hand away from his mouth. "And don't kick the seat."

The hand she uses contains a rolled-up handkerchief. Momentarily it presses against his skin, leaving a damp spot. Felix squeals and edges away.

"You little brat," she mutters, and moves as if to pinch him. Then she follows his gaze. She lowers her hand to her lap and smiles. It's not a proper smile, Felix thinks—it looks more like she's going to throw up.

"Looks like she's just about to kiss him, doesn't it?" she says, nodding at the window. "Well, she's not. That's not baby Jesus, you know. That's some other kid. That kid's been naughty in church. And Mary is just about to eat him."

"It's true," she nods in response to Felix's incredulous stare.

She glances around her, checking for eavesdroppers, as if she is about to impart a great secret, and leans in close to him. "And if you play up in church," she whispers in his ear, "she waits until night time, then she comes to life and climbs down out of that window and follows you home. She comes in through your bedroom window—even if it's shut and bolted, she just flows straight through, 'cos she's made of glass, remember—and she eats you all up. Crunch, crunch, crunch, with her big glass teeth."

Felix stops drumming his heels. Fear-fuelled tears fill his eyes, and his vision of the glass Virgin swims.

It's almost as if she is moving.

It has been a day of unmitigated crap. Sent home early without pay and with the very real possibility of having no job to return to in the morning, and now it's raining. Pissing down, actually. Still, the torrential downpour isn't enough to make Felix take the shortest route home. That would force him to walk past two churches. He wouldn't attempt that even on a good day.

He doesn't pause to dry off when he gets home, just goes directly to the kitchen and pours himself a couple of measures of bourbon. He downs it in one swallow. Water drips onto the battered linoleum floor and trickles off to hide in the cracks. Felix wishes he could do that; find the cracks in the world and crawl into them out of sight.

The phone rings, and he jumps, uttering a tiny startled 'eep'.

"Hello?... Oh, hello, Mum... Yeah, I came home early today. Wasn't feeling well... Yeah, no, I'll be alright... Lunch this Sunday? I dunno, Mum, I might be busy... Who told you about my new girlfriend? Clare? How would she know? I haven't spoken to Clare for... No, it's not like that, Mum, of course I'm not avoiding my family...NO!!! No, I can't meet you at church in the morning." His refusal comes out sharper than intended. He slumps into an armchair as he bears the brunt of his mother's inevitable guilt trip.

"The thing is, Mum, Harmony's a bit shy," he lies. "I don't think she would cope very well with the full-on family church and Sunday roast experience. How about we compromise? We could meet you at that little café round the corner for lunch. Save you from having to cook. It'll be my treat."

Negotiations concluded, Felix hangs up. He is suddenly aware of how cold he is in his wet clothes.

Fucking Clare, he thinks. Fucking meddling fucking spiteful fucking Clare.

"**P**ussy," Clare says scornfully. Clare hates having to look after Felix when Mum is out, which happens more and more often now that she has a new boyfriend. And Clare hates it even more when Felix cries, especially when he goes all red in the face and snot comes out of his nose in big green bubbles. Tears drip off his face and sting on contact with his bleeding knee.

"Do you think Jesus ever cried like that? Jesus never cried, not when he was a little boy, not even when they took him and whipped all the skin off his back and hammered big nails into his hands and feet." She grabs Felix by the ear, making him cry even louder, and drags him over to the picture on the wall of Jesus on the cross. He looks up at Jesus, and Jesus looks back, mournful and sympathetic.

"See? No tears. And you're sitting there carrying on over a little graze." She squats down and presses her cheek against his, and for a moment Felix thinks she is going to relent, going to comfort him.

"They don't even show you what they really did to him in that picture," she says. "It's too gross. You wouldn't even be able to look at it. It would make you chuck up your lunch. Shall I tell you? No? Too bad." She pinches the back of his neck, holding his head in place and forcing him to look at the picture. The tortures she describes seem to unfold in front of him. Jesus suffers. Jesus bleeds. What Jesus does not do is cry like a baby.

Pussy.

Without him asking her to, Harmony has dressed for the occasion. Minimal make up, dyed black hair tied back in a ponytail, the austerity of her long black skirt and Dr Martens boots tempered by a pastel pink shirt that makes her skin look sallow. To his mother and sister she is smilingly demure, polite and respectful. His mother appears to be completely taken in, but Clare watches Harmony intently throughout lunch with a sardonic smile on her face, poised to expose the lie at any moment.

When they stand to leave at the end of lunch, his mother takes Harmony's hands in hers and kisses her on the cheek.

"You've got a real keeper here, Felix," she says. "Make sure you look after her."

Clare stays seated. She leans back in her chair and cocks an eyebrow at Felix.

"Oh yes..." Clare says, "She's a real *angel*."

Felix's guts cramp up and threaten to disgorge his meal on the table. He breathes deeply, counts to ten, and summons up a mental image of his girlfriend naked on all fours with him taking her from behind. Harmony, an angel? No. Not that.

Anything but that.

No pets, his mum had said, the landlord wouldn't allow it, but this was just one tiny little mouse, purchased from the pet shop with his pocket money for fifty cents. The landlord need never know.

Except he had been playing with it in his room and it had gotten away from him, moving faster than he thought possible, and now it's lost God-knows-where in the house, and he has to find it before anyone else does.

A scream from the lounge tells him he is too late.

He runs into the lounge. Clare's no timid maiden standing on a chair in terror, oh no, she is taking immediate action. She picks up the nearest heavy object, which happens to be the family heirloom bible, and chases after the mouse, which zigzags evasively across the carpet.

"No, Clare, wait..."

Thud. Clare hammers the bible down squarely on top of the mouse. They both stop and stare at the floor. Felix's first instinct is to lift the weight off, see if he can mitigate the damage, as if there is some magical Five Second Rule of mortality. But with his shoulder sagging, he knows, the book's judgment is inexorable.

Clare wrinkles her nose and gingerly nudges the bible aside with her foot. They both recoil at the revealed sight of the crushed and bloody little corpse.

"What did you have to do that for?" Felix cries. "It wasn't hurting anybody! It was my pet!" He lunges at her, beating his fists against her chest, but she is far too big and strong for him. She shoves him away, hard enough to make him lose his balance and land with a painful bump on the floor.

She looms over him. "That wasn't a pet, Felix, that was vermin. But seeing as you're claiming it as *your* vermin, you can clean up this mess." She leans down and grabs the front of his T-shirt, pulling his face close to hers.

"Especially the bible. You better make sure there's not a trace of blood left on it. Or else you are going to burn in hell for sure."

Back in Harmony's room after lunch, Harmony strips off her pink shirt and hurls it into a corner with disgust.

"What the fuck was up with those two?" she asks, her voice muffled as she pulls a black T-shirt over her head. "Especially your sister? She's a real piece of work, isn't she?" Harmony puts on an insipid little girl voice, mocking Clare savagely. "'She's a real angel.' Fucking two-faced bitch." She flings herself backwards onto her bed.

Felix's eyes fill with tears. Clare was right all those years ago, he *is* a pussy, but he can't help himself. He stands at the foot of Harmony's bed and sobs. Harmony sits up, her furious scowl turning into a frown of concern.

"What is it, baby?"

So he tells her. Everything.

Felix hears something sounding like a bagful of tiny marbles being emptied onto the tiles in the kitchen. He goes to investigate, and finds Clare looking at the floor with a curiously thoughtful gaze, one hand still clutching the remnants of a string of pearls around her neck.

"Is that Mum's pearl necklace?" Felix says. "The one she inherited from Grandma? What happened?"

Clare shakes her head. "Never mind that," she says. "I want to show you something."

He folds his arms across his chest. "What is it? What could be more interesting than seeing you catch it from Mum? She'll be home in…"

"Half an hour," says Clare. "We've got half an hour." When Felix does not respond, she reaches into her pocket and draws out a small metal object on the end of a frayed piece of twine. "I've found the key to Dad's tool shed."

Felix gasps. He's been itching to get into that shed for years, but Mum declared it strictly off limits after Dad died, and it's sat undisturbed ever since.

"What are you waiting for, dickhead?" says Clare. "Let's go."

Once the shed door clicks shut behind them, Felix can only make out vague shapes in the gloom. He flicks the light switch up and down several times without a result. He hears Clare rummaging around behind him. There is a barely audible whoosh, and a circle of light appears to encompass them both. Clare moves to the far wall and sets the lit candle in her hand carefully down on a work bench. Felix scarcely has time to take in some of the tools hanging in their designated spots before Clare grabs him by the hand.

"Come over here," she says. "This is the best bit." She has both of his hands in hers now, and she walks backwards, smiling. She stops when her butt touches the work bench and moves to the side so Felix can see. He shrugs.

"So what?" he says. "It's just a vice."

"Oh, no," she says. "This isn't just any old vice." She runs her fingertips along the inside of the dust-coated jaws. "Here, feel this." Intrigued in spite of himself, Felix reaches out.

Before he realizes, Clare has grabbed his hands again, slipped his thumbs inside the vice, and spun the handle. He is trapped.

"What the… Clare? Clare! That hurts, Clare. Stop fucking around and let me go."

Clare tsk-tsks at the obscenity. "Do you know what the favourite torture device was in the Spanish Inquisition? Thumbscrews. People would confess to anything, even stuff that wasn't true, just to stop the pain." She jumps up to sit on the bench, lifts her rosary beads from around her neck and dangles them in front of Felix's face.

"Listen very carefully, sinner," she says. "I'm going to count through these beads, and with every 'Hail Mary' I'm going to tighten the screws. If you don't confess, your thumbs are going to turn to mush before I get halfway round. Now—who broke the necklace?"

"What are you talking about? You did!"

Click.

"Wrong answer."

Felix bites the inside of his mouth to keep from screaming. He will not give the mad bitch the satisfaction, he will not...

"I'll ask you again. Who broke the necklace?"

"I... I don't know what you want me to say, Clare... I don't know who broke it, I didn't see..."

Click.

"Close, but no cigar. Shall we try again?"

The agony is not confined to his thumbs, it only originates there and radiates upwards to infuse his entire body.

"Oh my God, Clare, please, stop, I'll do whatever you want, please..."

"Don't blaspheme, fucker."

Click.

"I did it! It was me! I broke it!" His words tumble out in barely articulate sobs.

Clare slides off the bench and releases the tension on the vice. Felix slumps to the floor and cradles his throbbing thumbs to his chest. Clare clasps his face in her hands and pats one cheek in a parody of sisterly affection. The rosary beads press into his skin, and he tries not to puke.

"That's what I wanted to hear," she says. She walks towards the door, then pauses and turns back to look at Felix.

"There are a lot of dangerous things in this shed," she muses. "Electric drills, saws, hammers, old tins of petrol—no wonder

Mum doesn't want us coming in here. A girl could do a lot of damage with some of this stuff. Wait 'til you're asleep, hit you when your defences are down...you know, just in case you're thinking of recanting."

Then she is gone, and Felix is left alone in the shadows, the ghost of clicking rosary beads sounding in his ears.

"I know what you need to do." Harmony's voice, whispered in Felix's ear, is ragged with lust.

"What?" He is close to coming, barely able to register her words. She grasps his hips, slows his thrusts, edges him back from the brink.

"You need to burn down a church."

"Wh...what?!?" He had half-expected her to suggest counselling. This insane idea nearly shrivels his cock inside her. He tries to pull away, but she has him held fast, her legs wrapped tightly around his waist.

"Think of it," she whispers. Her hips grind up to meet his. "Imagine how therapeutic it would be...all those symbols of repression and pain, going up in flames..."

She increases the tempo and draws him closer, pressing her chest to his. His arousal mounts in spite of himself.

Suddenly, yes, he can picture it, a purifying wall of fire obliterating all his fears. He drives himself onward to his climax, oblivious now to Harmony writhing beneath him, the roar of blaze in his ears drowning out his own cries of release.

Even in the dark...no, especially in the dark, with the street lamps casting sinister shadows, the church is a monument of terror. It's as if the building is protected by an invisible force field, the weight of which presses on Felix's chest with every step he takes towards it. Harmony leads him by the hand, not to the front door, but into the darkness down the side of the church. She squeezes through a gap left by a broken fence paling and tugs Felix in after her. Unerringly—she has scoped out the target well in advance—she leads him to a small door at the rear of the church. Felix stops on the threshold and leans over, gasping, with his hands on his knees.

"I don't think I can do this…"

"Ssh." Harmony presses a forefinger to his lips. "Relax. Close your eyes, if it helps. Now hang on a minute while I pick this lock."

Felix does as he is told and squeezes his eyes shut, focusing on the gentle rustles, clinks and scrapes of Harmony taking tools from her backpack and applying them to the lock.

"We're in," Harmony whispers. Again she takes his hand and drags him in her wake.

The aroma of dust and incense inside the church nearly sends him running. Oblivious to his distress, Harmony stalks down the aisle, the light from her torch flitting erratically around the interior. Pews. Altar. Candles. Font. Blessed Virgin. Confessional. Stations of the Cross. Each is illuminated for a split second in a dizzying, horrific slide show. He covers his face with his hands and swallows the bile rising in the back of his throat.

He feels tugging on the backpack he wears, hears a faint splashing sound and breathes in fumes as Harmony coats the interior of the church with petrol. Child-like, Harmony giggles.

"I've always wanted to do this."

"What—commit arson?" A distant part of himself marvels at his ability to be acerbic at a time like this.

"Yeah," she replies, without a trace of irony. He is abruptly, painfully aware of how wrong this is, how wrong *she* is. He wonders distantly, how did this happen? How did I get here, to this place, this moment, with this woman?

"Here," she says, pushing something into his hands. "You have to do this." He opens his eyes and looks down at the lighter in his hand. He flicks the wheel experimentally with his thumb, once, twice. It catches alight on the third spin. Beyond the flickering flame he sees a stained-glass window bearing the image of the Virgin Mary and child. Just like the one in his childhood church, he thinks. The Blessed Virgin wavers in the light.

Crunch, crunch, crunch, with her big glass teeth.

Felix starts with a jolt of fear. The lighter tumbles from his suddenly nerveless fingers. The flame ignites the petrol and spreads with surprising speed.

"Oh, shit," Harmony mutters next to him. "Shit…"

He follows her gaze. She has forgotten to leave a break in her petrol trail, and the way out is cut off by the fire.

"C'mon, Felix, we've got to go. Now!"

He hears a shout from the rear of the church. A grey-haired man advances on them, his long robe swirling about his legs. At first glance the robe looks like a priest's cassock, and Felix stumbles backward away from the man. Then he realizes that it is a long dressing gown. The man beckons and says something. His words are drowned out by the roar of the blaze.

Felix looks at the route he must take to escape. Past the altar, past the confessional, past the statue of a crucified and bleeding Christ…

He falls to his knees. Harmony grabs his arm and hauls, but she is too slight to move him. With a final despairing glance, she runs and leaps the flames to land safely in the arms of her rescuer.

The heat is punishing now. Smoke stings his eyes and invades his lungs. Hymn books curl and blacken. Burnt pages float towards the ceiling on currents of hot air. Flames pay obeisance at the feet of Christ, who looks impassively on.

Felix leans over, his forehead nearly touching the floor, and coughs, his body going into spasms with the effort. His eyes water, only for the tears to evaporate almost instantly.

Do you think Jesus ever cried like that?

Felix bows in an obscene parody of prayer at the foot of the altar, which is now entirely engulfed in flame. That must be what the devil's altar must look like, Felix thinks. He stares, paralysed with terror, as the altar collapses on itself. A shower of sparks sprinkles over him like confetti. He edges backwards, only to meet a wall of flame at his heels. He wails as his sleeve catches alight and the cheap synthetic fabric melts onto his skin. All that remains is for him to crawl into a foetal position and wait for the inevitable.

You are going to burn in hell for sure.

The Shadow Over Tarehu Cove

Renee's stomach turned as her wife Marika threw their little hatchback into the turns on the narrow country road. They were halfway to Marika's family marae to attend a tangi, and it had just occurred to Renee that she'd never attended a funeral. Of course, she had known grief and loss, from losing childhood pets to a handful of heartbreaks from failed relationships prior to meeting Marika, but her friends had always enjoyed robust good health and fortune, and incredibly there had been no deaths in her family since she was a baby. Accompanying Marika to farewell her grandmother, not only did she have to contend with the unfamiliar protocol of a three-day tangi in the company of mostly strangers, but in supporting her wife in her grief, she would be navigating treacherous waters. Not one for extravagant displays of emotion at the best of times, Marika tended to retreat inside herself when enduring great stress or turmoil, like a wounded animal hiding in a cave, and it was Renee's job to venture in after her and coax her back out—preferably without getting bitten in the process. If she were to be honest with herself, Marika's guardedness was partly what drew Renee to her; she had been both challenged by her reserve and rewarded when she became one of the elite few to break through it.

Renee glanced at her wife in profile, Marika's expression inscrutable, and her queasiness intensified. For better or for worse, that's what she had signed up for, hadn't she? She looked back to the road and braced herself for another blind corner.

Renee barely knew Marika's grandmother, and found the tangi emotionally exhausting. She could only imagine how hard it was for Marika. She'd been uncomfortable at the thought of sleeping in the same room as a dead body, but that apprehension was put to rest with more practical concerns of sharing her sleeping space with dozens of snoring, farting strangers. She slept lightly, waking often, while the songs and speeches carried on through the night.

Occasionally during the day she wandered into the kitchen, picked up a tea towel or a potato peeler and made vague efforts to help out, but mostly she made an effort to stay away from the others. Marika's family wasn't openly hostile or deliberately rude, but they had a way of flowing around and away from her, making space for her only temporarily, and grudgingly, as if she were a foreign body cast into the stream of their busy lives.

The morning of the interment dawned misty and unseasonably cool. Renee prepared herself as best she could in the shower block, peering into the mirror above the hand basins to apply makeup. They changed shoes for the walk up the paddock to the cemetery. Marika took Renee's hand, the first prolonged touch they'd shared in a couple of days, and they took up a position near the head of the funeral procession. By the time they reached the graveside, Renee's palm was sweaty in Marika's grip.

Somebody began to keen, a mournful sound that made Renee uncomfortable. Marika rested her head on Renee's shoulder and relaxed enough to share her bottled emotions. She sobbed, her tears soaking into Renee's suit jacket. The bush-shrouded hills, the swirling mist, the moist air carrying a hint of salt from the coast, so alien from the diesel and dust and concrete of the city she was used to, threatened to drown her. As the wailing intensified with more women taking up the call, and the priest intoned his final words, Renee swayed on her feet. Marika's arm tensed to keep her upright, and for a moment it was Marika having to prop her up, not the other way around.

With the formalities over, there was still some business to which Marika needed to attend. Renee managed to persuade her to book into a motel rather than prevail on the further hospitality of family. There was only one choice within a fifty-kilometre radius, a little sixteen-room affair adjacent to the local pub. Both establishments looked like they were stuck in a 1970s time warp. While Marika did her thing—she could not be persuaded to let Renee tag along—Renee read, napped, grazed on stale packaged snacks from the service station nearby, and made a desultory attempt at exercise by assuming a few yoga poses, before abandoning the endeavour for want of a yoga mat. The prospect of a pub dinner that night had never seemed more enticing.

Carrying her third mixed drink back from the bar, Renee approached the table and found Marika talking with another woman. Renee saw the newcomer brush a fingertip across the back of her wife's hand. Renee was drunk and in no mood to behave civilly. Rather than risk making an arse of herself, she retreated to a corner of the bar to nurse her pride.

A thin old woman nearby was staring at her. Renee was surprised when the woman spoke.

"You studied at Miskatonic University." It was a statement, not a question, delivered in a slurred yet surprisingly authoritative voice.

Renee blinked, wondering how this stranger would know that. The old woman held out her hand and Renee felt obliged to hold it.

"They call me Kitty, Aunty Kitty to my face, Crazy Kitty behind my back." Her grin spread further, her eyes sinking into folds of skin, her body shaking with soundless laughter. "I was visited by bigwigs from Miskatonic once, ya know. When I was a kid. Want to know why?" Her demeanour shifted, no longer jovial. She leaned close to Renee and fixed her with an almost desperate stare. Renee smelled alcohol, unwashed flesh, and a hint of cow shit.

"Umm ..." Renee leaned away and cast her gaze over to Marika, hoping that she might come to her rescue, but Marika was still talking to the other woman, oblivious to Renee's absence. Kitty waved a near-empty glass under Renee's nose, and she was grateful for the comparatively wholesome scent of yeast and hops.

"Buy me a drink, and I'll tell ya."

Her wife's companion whispered in Marika's ear, eliciting a laugh and a playful shoulder bump. It looked like nobody was going to save her from Crazy Kitty any time soon. With a resigned nod, Renee took the proffered vessel and headed for the bar.

Renee had found the term: "non-US ethnic minorities only" somewhat patronizing for a Kiwi teenager with limited life experience and modest family means. Nevertheless, she convinced herself that a scholarship to an overseas university was too great an opportunity to disregard. She had been delighted to learn her application was successful, and she spent the months between acceptance and arrival in Arkham fantasizing about how amazing her stay was going to be.

Even before she'd arrived at Arkham she made a new friend, a young Indigenous Australian woman named Jida whom she met at the bus terminal, and who was attending Miskatonic on the same scholarship. Alongside this new companion, her arrival in the university town built beside the Miskatonic River, with its Gothic architecture, was just as she'd pictured it, but that was about where fantasy and reality parted ways. They'd barely stepped off the bus when they were set upon by rich white boys (that being the dominant demographic of the student body) to join this club or that, most of which were esoteric in nature. One tall, earnest young man with an abnormally high forehead strode up to Jida.

"Are you the Maori girl taking marine biology?" He pronounced it 'may-OR-rye', and Renee suppressed a wince; no doubt he wouldn't be the only one to mangle the word. Jida pointed over her shoulder at Renee.

"You've got to join the cryptozoology club," he said to Renee, looming over her. "You simply must." Then, to Jida. "You too, I suppose, maybe, if you want."

"Why not?" Jida had said with a shrug and a smile. "It could be good for a laugh."

At first, the two brown-skinned women from the Antipodes were the subjects of intense scrutiny. The other members grilled them on various aspects of their culture, in particular their knowledge of the creatures of their myths and legends. Jida strung them along for months, spinning fanciful tales that bore little resemblance to real Dreamtime stories, and weaving in hints of extra-terrestrial encounters and alien abductions that seemed to greatly excite the group. Renee lacked the imagination to play the same game, all her answers being variations on: "That's just a story—it's not meant to be taken literally" and "I don't know anything about that." If the truth be known, she found the earnestness of the other members, and their deep longing to believe, a childish and unnerving trait in young adults who were meant to be aspiring scientists and scholars. Yet she lingered in the club long after the others lost interest in her, for reasons she was never fully able to articulate.

Outside of the club, the local students viewed them with a certain degree of resentment, their scholarships being perceived as an undeserved 'free ride.' Rather than her horizons broadening, Renee found her world shrinking. She seldom ventured further than the lecture hall, library, and the dilapidated accommodation wing in which the administration corralled all the foreign scholarship students.

Jida transferred back to an Australian university at the end of the first year.

"Sorry, darl, this place gives me the shits," she'd said as she kissed a tearful Renee goodbye.

Following that, Renee felt adrift. She managed to stick it out and complete her degree, but it was more out of a lack of anything better to do than a true drive for achievement. Upon returning to her home soil, she all but wept in relief, and soon put conscious thought of the oppressive atmosphere of Miskatonic Uni out of her mind. She must have taken in more than she thought during her time in the crypto club, though. Any chance she got, and even for some opportunities she manufactured, she would talk at length about yetis and Bigfoot and other such creatures, until she gained a reputation as being 'a bit of an odd fish.' Eventually she learned to keep that strand of specialised knowledge to herself.

Now here she was, over a decade later, in a fusty old country pub at the arse end of the world, catapulted back to her memories of those early days at Miskatonic by a chance meeting with the local nut job.

"...they wanted to know about the *Ponaturi*."

"Huh, what?" Renee was barely listening to Kitty. Marika must have finally noticed Renee's absence and looked around the bar for her; both she and her friend were staring at Renee. Marika scowled and gave an exaggerated head shake, a pantomimed warning: don't stand too close to the crazy lady, it might be catching. In a drunken act of defiance, Renee lifted her chin and pointedly turned away.

"The *Ponaturi*. I saw them take my cousin from the beach. Took her to their underwater caves, and we never saw her again. They might have taken me, too, 'cept I was only little, and I ran and hid under a log. I can still remember it—me tucked in tight in the dirt, and those ugly fuckers snuffling and shuffling through the bush trying to sniff me out..." For a moment Kitty looked lost in her recollections, her rheumy gaze distant and her half-empty glass threatening to slip from suddenly slack fingers. Then she shuddered and brought herself back to the present. "It happened at Tarehu Cove. You ask your girly over there about it." Kitty nodded towards Marika. "Only land access to that beach is over her family farm. 'Course, she'll probably tell you it's bullshit, but she knows." She gestured to encompass the patrons of the bar. "They all know," she muttered in a tone laced with bitterness. She drained her glass in one swallow, thrust it into Renee's hand and smacked her lips together wetly. The sound made Renee queasy. Everything was making her queasy—the press of poorly washed bodies, Marika's distance, the excess of booze she'd consumed, Kitty's incomprehensible tale—and she had to hold onto the bar, close her eyes and take several deep breaths before she was able to order another beer for Kitty. Marika had spoken fondly and often of the secluded little cove she had frequented in her youth, but Ponaturi? She had no idea what that was about...

Except you've heard that word before, haven't you, Renee? In a dusty room in a far-off land, mispronounced by American accents. You've heard the word, listened to the stories, imagined the stench

and the slimy touch of their amphibian limbs, dreamt of the creature's
loathsome faces, and woken up screaming…

Renee elbowed her way back through the crowd and held the
beer out to Kitty. At the same time, someone took hold of her
other arm in an ungentle grip. Renee yelped, startled, and nearly
spilled the beer. It was Marika, looking grim. The woman she'd
been talking to was nowhere to be seen.

"It's late. I'm tired. Let's go," Marika said. She glared at Kitty
and began to steer Renee away.

"Wait!" The old woman clutched at Renee. For a moment she
was caught in a tug-of-war. Just before Marika could wrench her
free, Kitty leaned in and whispered in Renee's ear:

"If you go down to Tarehu Cove, make sure you don't stay
past dark."

L ying skin to skin in bed with Marika, alone at last after what
felt like weeks, Renee should have been feeling amorous, but
couldn't summon up the energy. Still, her hand crept across
Marika's chest to idly toy with her nipple. Marika exhaled softly
and shifted to press a little more closely against her.

"That old woman in the bar, Kitty…" Renee began. "She tells
me you know something about the Ponaturi."

Marika's mood turned icy in an instant. She grabbed Renee's
wrist and pulled her hand away from its ministrations. "Don't,"
she commanded.

"Don't what?"

"Don't start with that crypto shit. We're here so I can spend
time with my whanau, not so you can indulge in your weird little
hobby."

Renee forced a laugh. "Oh, no, of course not. I only mentioned
it because…well, she's a bit loony, that Kitty, isn't she? Lucky
you came to get me when you did, otherwise I might never have
gotten away from her."

A pause, then a non-committal, "Hmmm." Marika's face was
unreadable in the dark, but she must have accepted the excuse;
she relaxed back against the mattress and released Renee's wrist,
then turned on her side with her back to Renee. Renee contented

herself with draping her arm over Marika's waist.

"Hey, I've got an idea," she murmured against Marika's neck. "We're not in a big hurry to head home tomorrow, are we? Why don't you show me that cove you've told me about? The one that the tourists can't find? It sounds really romantic..."

"Yeah... Yeah, okay, I'd like that."

Minutes later, Marika was asleep, a state that was much later coming for Renee. She should have been looking forward to a seaside tryst with her soul mate—so now that it was confirmed, why did the prospect of visiting Tarehu Cove infuse her with dread?

They slept late the next day, and when they woke, Marika was in a much better mood, toying with Renee's feet under the table at brunch and flirting with the shop assistant at the general store to secure a small discount off the two gaudy beach towels they purchased. The drive to the beach took them off tarsealed roads and onto several winding kilometres of gravel that challenged their urban vehicle's suspension, then onto a long dirt track that led ultimately to a padlocked farm gate bearing a hand-painted "Private Property—Keep Out" sign. The sign writer had used too-thin red paint and the letters had run slightly, making the warning appear fresh and bloody. Marika pulled on the hand brake and got out, winking at Renee through the windscreen as she approached the gate; not at the padlocked end where logic dictated it would open with a key, but at the opposite end. She hefted the gate off its hinges and swung it open.

"We all got sick of trying to keep track of the keys, so Aroha came up with that idea," she explained when she got back into the car.

"Aroha?"

Marika dismissed the query with a wave. "She's a cousin..."

Who isn't around here? Renee thought sourly. As if on cue, a figure appeared on a small hill in the distance. As it grew closer, it resolved into a young woman riding a bay mare at a gallop. Just when it looked like they might vault the bonnet, the woman reined the horse in sharply. Renee recognised her as the woman talking to Marika in the bar the night before.

Marika's introductions were made more awkward with Aroha looking imperiously down on them from astride her mount. The woman was dressed in a faded T-shirt dotted with holes, black shorts and grubby gumboots. She rode bareback, her muscular thighs gripping the horse's sides, her long and untamed black hair stirring, Medusa-like, in the breeze. If it weren't for her tatty attire, she might have resembled a warrior princess bent on striking down a rival.

"We're heading down to the beach," Marika told Aroha. "Renee wanted to see it." She looked sideways at Renee, smiled and took her hand. At this display of affection, Aroha stiffened, sending her horse skittering slightly. Renee smiled smugly back.

"Didn't happen to bring your dive gear, did ya?" Aroha asked. Marika shook her head.

"I've got *one* spare set," that emphasis on *one*, green eyes flicking towards Renee and away. "Come out on the boat if you want. It'll be just like old times." Another pointed glance at Renee, meaning: *there is no place for you here*.

"Thanks, but nah. We're just after a bit of alone time." Marika squeezed Renee's hand.

"Yeah, well..." Aroha jerked her head in the direction from which she came, indicating a long, single-level dwelling positioned for panoramic sea views. "You know where to find me if you change your mind."

The track to the beach traversed a couple of kilometres of gorse-studded paddock before disappearing into dense bushland. The final stretch had to be travelled on foot. Laden with towels and picnic supplies, they picked their way carefully through the undergrowth for several hundred metres, following a creek on a gentle downward slope.

They emerged abruptly from the bush onto sand. Renee stumbled and righted herself, almost breathless as she caught the first sight of the glittering and boundless stretch of sea. The beach was tiny and pristine, a horseshoe-shaped sliver of paradise, delicate wavelets lapping the shore. A pohutukawa tree in full bloom jutted from a small cliff, providing just enough shade for two. Beyond that cliff, Marika had told her, lay another much larger beach, easily accessible at low tide and also frequented by Marika and her cousins. But Renee had little interest in exploring the other side, not when this spot seemed crafted just for them.

Marika was already stripping off, leaving her clothes in a trail to the ocean's edge as she whooped and squealed in a childlike rush to dive beneath the water. She came up gasping and laughing, clutching her arms across her bare chest in a futile gesture of self-protection.

"What's it like?" Renee called.

"Fucking freezing!" Marika called back, before throwing herself backwards into the brine again.

Renee was more cautious to get in—most of her underwater activities were undertaken in a five-millimetre wetsuit, and she was too well schooled in the dangers of hypothermia to take the chill lightly—but soon the sun, the solitude and Marika's infectious delight had her acclimatised and splashing with glee alongside her lover.

Sometime later hunger called. They ate as they had bathed, completely naked, towelling off only enough to keep salt water from dripping onto their food, and letting the air dry them completely. When Marika finished eating, she smoothed out her towel and reclined on it with a sigh, arching her back to press her breasts and belly skyward, then fell back into stillness with her eyes closed.

Renee took a moment to drink the sight in—small conical breasts, smooth brown skin stretched over lean muscle and classically sculpted cheekbones, large, bony hands and feet that earned her much teasing from friends and family but only drew Renee's admiration, for their implications of strength and capability. *And mine, all mine.* Renee's gaze wandered up from those hands—and thoughts of what Marika could do with them—to her mouth, lips slightly parted in a contented smile, made Renee smile too.

"You've got a crumb on you," Renee said. "Right...here." She leaned over and kissed the corner of Marika's mouth. She began to draw away, and Marika caught her. With a giggle, Marika rolled, pulling Renee over until their positions were reversed and Marika had Renee pinned beneath her. Marika kissed her back, open-mouthed and desperate, almost violent in her desire, and it was Renee's turn to arch up, offering herself to Marika's heat.

Renee woke to a moment of disorientation. Her mouth was dry, and everything ached—had they been drinking? Then her memory kicked in. They'd made love on the beach, and it had been urgent, vigorous, transcendent. Then they must have fallen asleep. Now it was dark, she was cold, sand was stuck and scratching in delicate places, and she needed to pee.

Marika had managed to cocoon herself in both beach towels. She breathed heavily, not quite snoring. A sudden, sharp surge of tenderness speared Renee, and she left her wife to sleep on. Moonlight showed their scattered belongings only as vague, shadowy lumps. Renee felt about the beach until she found shoes and a T-shirt, and made her way bare-assed up the beach to find an appropriate spot in the bush to urinate. It was strange, she mused as she squatted and released control on her bladder, how deep one's conditioning went; she knew they were alone and there was next to no chance they'd be disturbed, and she'd been only too happy to have sex in the open air, but the minute she had to take a leak, here she was taking the trouble to hide behind a tree.

Two things intruded on her senses at once: a soft splashing sound, at first indistinguishable from the splatter of urine on the ground, and a faint but repugnant odour of rotting fish. Both came from the direction of the beach, and Renee peered around the tree trunk in search of the cause.

Someone...no, some*thing* stood on the beach. It was a humanoid shape, but only superficially; its head was too narrow, its eyes too bulging, its posture too distorted, and its hands and feet were webbed, unlike any human Renee had ever seen. Its belly gleamed palely in the moonlight, the rest of its scaly flesh a darker hue, and its back bore a stubby dorsal ridge.

The creature turned and gave a croaking bark, and on its signal, several more narrow heads arose from the water. Renee counted five, seven, eleven…they kept on coming, emerging from the sea until some two dozen of the things stood on the sand. Their fishy stench flooded the air, and Renee choked back a retch. A burst of adrenaline zinged through her body, urging fight or flight. Or freeze.

Renee stood rigidly still, pressed against the tree trunk as if she sought to sink into it, and all but held her breath. The creatures hopped and shambled and loped up the beach, their misshapen feet slapping obscenely on the sand; heading straight for Marika.

They swarmed to surround her, and stood looking down on her for a few moments. Then two of them bent to grab her and haul her to her feet. Renee cried out, suddenly heedless of her own survival, but she was drowned out by the screams of Marika herself, who was suddenly wide-awake and struggling. The towels fell, revealing her nakedness, and the creatures bayed and hooted with what might have been appreciation, or lust.

Another two took hold of Marika's legs, and they lifted her off her feet. She bucked and writhed against their grip. Several more shuffled forward to take hold of her at various points along her limbs. Renee imagined their putrid, clammy touch, and retched anew. Now Marika was virtually immobilized and held aloft, facing the moon like an offering. They carried her in this fashion into the sea until they stood waist deep in the water, with a whimpering Marika floating on her back in their midst. Two of the monsters at the head of the procession took deep, chest-inflating breaths. One of them bent to press a lipless mouth to Marika's. She fought it, but it wrapped a hank of her hair in one webbed claw to hold her in place.

When Renee realized what they intended, it broke the spell on her fear-frozen limbs; she sprinted from her hiding place towards the sea; too late. They dived with eerie synchronicity, taking Marika under with them. When Renee reached the water's edge, not even bubbles remained to mark their passing.

She was lucky not to break a limb in her frantic, stumbling passage through the bush and back to the car, and lucky not to completely lose her mind as she scrabbled through the bundle of belongings she'd swept up from the beach in the search for the keys. After far too long, her fingers closed on cool metal. She set the car on the straightest line for Aroha's house on the hill, headless of dips or bumps or gorse, the wild ride jolting her dangerously in her seat until she connected with a rudimentary driveway that provided a smoother path.

She was still pounding on Aroha's front door when it opened. Aroha appeared annoyed at the disturbance at first, but at the sight of Renee, her eyes widened and she took a step back.

"What the—?"

Renee looked down at herself and realized the cause of her shock; in her rush, she'd paused only to put on underpants, and blood streaked her bare legs from several scratches and scrapes she'd sustained running through the bush. She shook her head.

"It's Marika. They took Marika! We have to go get her back."

"Just, just slow down, calm down. Who took Marika?"

"I don't know, the...the frog fish men things. The Ponaturi!"

Aroha stared at Renee in silence.

"I'm not crazy!" Renee blurted. "I know what I saw!"

More silence. Then, quietly, sadly, as she began to turn away—"I can't help you."

"Wait!" Renee grabbed Aroha's arm and played her trump card. "You love her, don't you?"

A range of emotions played over Aroha's face. After a lengthy pause, she sighed.

"Alright. Come in. But you have to understand —it'll be dangerous, and a long shot. No guarantees we'll be able to save her, and we'll have to wait until tomorrow night. They only come to shore after dark, so that's when we're most likely to find her unguarded."

"Okay, okay, whatever you say," Renee said, nodding furiously. She started to follow Aroha inside, then stopped. "But how do you even know where to start looking? They took her into the ocean, for fuck's sake! She could be fucking anywhere!"

Her plan to charge after Marika and her captors, all guns blazing into the sea to mount a rescue was looking more and more nebulous by the minute.

Aroha barked a short, mirthless laugh. "Oh, that's the easy part. We'll find her in the place where we know not to go."

Aroha cleared a space for her in a spare bedroom. "Sleep, you're going to need it," she commanded, but that proved impossible. Renee lay awake through the night torturing herself, her mind filled with thoughts of what might be happening to Marika. Dawn saw her jittery with nerves and sleeplessness. Aroha, on the other hand, seemed unnaturally calm, cooking breakfast with little conversation and pushing a plate laden with bacon, fried eggs, baked beans and butter-soaked toast in front of Renee. She supervised Renee while she ate as if she were a child, ensuring she cleaned her plate, then left her to do god-knows-what while Renee paced and fidgeted and stared out the lounge window at the sea.

Aroha returned close to dusk in a battered ute, the bed of which was laden with assorted dive gear. "I had to ask around and borrow some extra stuff," she explained. "I don't normally go out on night dives."

They drove a short distance to a large storage shed where Aroha's own dive equipment was kept. Under Aroha's instruction, Renee loaded up wetsuits, tanks, fins and the like, while Aroha attached a small dinghy with an outboard motor to the ute's towbar. They drove in the direction Renee had come from the night before, only to veer off and follow a path alongside the trees until they reached the far end of the bush. A short, steep descent took them straight onto a large stretch of beach.

"You guys were just around there," Aroha pointed to the left.

They suited up in silence. The spare wetsuit belonged to Aroha's younger brother, and was a touch too big for Renee, but the belt adjusted snugly enough. With weights, torch, dive knife and spear gun attached, it felt heavier than she was accustomed to. They launched the dinghy and set off diagonally from the beach, angling towards the little bay where Marika was last seen, the boat's motor intrusively loud. After several minutes, Aroha shut it off.

"Best not advertise that we're coming," she whispered as she took up a set of oars.

Even the soft splash of the oars seemed too noisy for Renee. After perhaps half an hour, Aroha stopped and dropped an anchor.

"Just stick close behind me," she instructed. Then she was tipping backwards out of the dinghy. Renee did as she was told and followed hot on her heels.

Under normal circumstances, Renee would feel at home and at ease underwater; her love of diving was a partial influence on her decision to study marine biology. Tonight, though, the weight of the water made her claustrophobic, the darkness beyond her torch beam was ominous, and the muted sound of her own breath was panic-inducing. To calm her racing nerves she narrowed her focus, concentrating only on keeping Aroha's fins an arm's distance from her mask.

They followed a steady downward trajectory until they swam parallel to and a few metres above the seabed. Even to her experienced eye, the submarine terrain looked largely featureless, and she wondered what criteria Aroha was navigating by. Eventually Aroha stopped and turned to face her. She pointed down at what looked like a slab of rock flush with the sand, and gestured to Renee to follow her. Puzzled, Renee did so. As they drew closer, she saw through the optical illusion; there was a gap between the rock and the sea bottom, just high enough to admit the pair. They slowed their pace as they entered the gap and travelled along a narrow, rocky tunnel. Renee's anxiety mounted with every second.

The roof of the tunnel abruptly gave way to open water, and they finned up to find themselves in a large, air-filled cavern, the walls of which were daubed in an unidentifiable phosphorescence that gave off a dim, almost welcoming glow. They hauled themselves out of the water and shrugged off their tanks, masks, regulators and fins.

"God, it stinks in here!" Aroha held her hand over her mouth and nose and spoke in a whisper, yet her voice echoed off the walls. Renee shushed her, and pointed at the closer of two corridors that led from the cavern; it was as good a place as any to begin their search.

They tiptoed along the passageway, briefly inspecting the half dozen large rooms that opened off it. At a guess, Renee would have called them living quarters, furnished as they were with objects made of unrecognisable substances and not configured for human bodies. Thankfully, the rooms were devoid of life.

They retraced their steps and moved to the entrance of the second corridor. The stench was even stronger here, and Renee was almost overwhelmed by the instinct to turn tail and swim for her life away from the uncanny place, but a faint, distinctly human and distinctly feminine whimper overrode that impulse. She pushed past Aroha and ran down the corridor, her only conscious thought to follow the sound.

She found Marika at the end of the passageway in a cavern larger than the others. Her wife lay curled up on her side on top of a great stone slab positioned in the centre of the room. Except for the slab (there was something vaguely altar-like about it, which would make Marika the offering, a thought that Renee shunned from her mind the moment it arose), the room was empty. Here, the phosphorescent walls were overlaid with decoration, alien artworks that were at once exquisite and repellent. She didn't dare examine them too closely; just glimpsing them out of the corner of her eye made her head swim and her gorge rise.

Gingerly, as if she might disintegrate at any moment, Renee ran her hands over Marika's body. Her face was partially obscured by her hair, and she made no move to register Renee's presence, only continued her soft, plaintive whimpering. Her skin was slick with some clear, viscous substance. Renee sniffed at her fingers and recoiled, gagging; it reeked of the Ponaturi.

Aroha had caught up with her, and stood warily at the entrance to the cavern. "Is she okay?"

"She's alive," Renee replied. "No bleeding or broken bones that I can tell. But no, she's far from okay." She manoeuvred Marika to a sitting position, then onto her feet. When prompted,

Marika moved willingly enough, but seemed completely without volition. Her eyes were wide and unfocused. It was if her mind and spirit had been drained from her, leaving only a beautiful shell.

They half-steered, half-carried Marika down the corridor, and were mere metres from the exit, when three Ponaturi stepped from another room to block their path. The two groups stared at each other for a couple of tense seconds, neither party expecting company. Then the Ponaturi charged.

Aroha, dive knife in hand and face twisted in fury, ran to meet them. All four tumbled back into the room from which the fish men had come.

Renee didn't wait to see the outcome. She dragged Marika past the melee, hauled on her dive gear faster than she would have thought possible, and jumped into the water with Marika in her arms, the cries of battle instantly muted as the brine closed over their heads. For one heart-stopping moment she thought that Marika's mind might be too damaged for her to know to hold her breath underwater, but that much of an instinct at least remained. Renee held her close and swam slowly, buddy-breathing all the way out through the underwater tunnel and back to the surface.

Mercifully, the dinghy had held on its anchor. Towing Marika's limp form through the water was one thing, getting her into the boat without capsizing was another much more difficult undertaking, and all the while Renee remained hyper-alert for signs of pursuit. After much dragging and cajoling, however, she had Marika stowed in a foetal ball in the bottom of the dinghy. With no further need for stealth, she powered the boat full throttle back to shore.

She did not speak of the events of that night. At first she felt guilty for abandoning Aroha, but soon she convinced herself that there had been no other way; Aroha knew better than she had what they were in for, had even warned her of the danger, and if she'd stopped to help, it would have only resulted in three women held captive in the Ponaturi's lair. Besides (the dark thought lurked), the way Marika had been flirting with Aroha, Renee felt ready to hand her over to the Ponaturi anyway.

For weeks afterwards she anticipated a knock on the door, a visit from authorities: we're investigating the disappearance of this woman, what can you tell us about that? But the visit never eventuated, and why would it? Most likely, someone in the family found the dinghy she'd abandoned on the beach, noticed the missing dive gear, and put some of the pieces of the puzzle together. They would have closed ranks and kept quiet.

They know. They all know...

Marika never emerged from her near-catatonic state, not even when she went into labour nine months later, so her baby boy was delivered by caesarean. Casual acquaintances assumed that Renee was the biological mother with the child conceived through fertility treatments, or that he was adopted, and that Marika's mysterious mind wipe was a tragic coincidence. Those closer, if they suspected the truth, did not pry.

The boy—Renee named him Matiu, the irony of which she did not discover until months later—was robustly healthy from birth, and hit all the right developmental milestones slightly ahead of schedule. Still, Renee could not help but wonder what might be developing in his half-alien mind. She hired a nanny to care for both mother and son while she worked, but none of them ever stayed for more than a month or two, and none could meet her eyes when they tendered their resignation. Perhaps it was the nauseating odour of rotting fish that clung to everything in the apartment no matter how thoroughly it was cleaned or what manner of perfumes were used to disguise it. Or perhaps it was Matiu's odd appearance that drove them away. He had none of his mother's good looks; his head was abnormally narrow, his eyes bulged unnaturally, his nose was so flat as to be almost non-existent, and his skin was peculiarly rough for such a young infant.

His strange looks certainly made her think equally strange and decidedly un-maternal thoughts. The thoughts were most intense when she was bathing him (and even bath time was weird, as he would only tolerate cold water with a full cup of salt added). With his spindly limbs giving off that smell, his unnerving, bug-eyed gaze fixed on hers, and with his mother sitting slack-jawed and staring at nothing, she often had the urge to put the pair of them in the car, drive them to the coast, and abandon them to the care of the creatures who had made them so.

Other times, the impulse was simpler, clearer, and more primal: maybe I should push his head under the water and hold him there. Just to see what will happen.

Story Publishing History

Breaking Windows—published in *Aurealis* September 2015

The Truth About Dolphins—published in *Disquiet* anthology September 2014

Wooden Heart—published in *Next* anthology April 2013

Ugly—not previously published

Q is for Quackery—published in *The Grimorium Verum* anthology February 2015

The Accession of Stinky—published in *Moonlight Tuber* September 2011

The Changing Tree—published in *Bards and Sages Quarterly* April 2012

The Oldest Profession—published in *Horror Library Vol 5* anthology November 2013

Drive, She Said—published in *Lovecraft e-zine* May 2012. Reprinted in *Making the Cut* anthology March 2014

Father Figure—published in *For the Night is Dark* anthology April 2013. Reprinted in *Memento Mori* anthology January 2017

Riding The Storm—published in *Disquiet* anthology September 2014

Slither and Squeeze—published in *Shifters* charity anthology June 2013. Reprinted in *Siren's Call* e-zine February 2019

Life In Miniature—published in *Big Pulp* December 2010. Reprinted in *Scared: Ten Tales of Horror* June 2012

The Witch's Library—published in *A Mythos Grimmly* anthology October 2015

The Long Way Home—not previously published

Late for Eisheth—published in *Demonologica Biblica* anthology March 2013

Symbols of Damnation—published in *Phobophobia* anthology December 2011.

Shadow over Tarehu Cove—published in *Cthulhu: Land of the Long White Cloud* anthology (IFWG Publishing Australia) September 2018